GRAVE HOMECOMING

A MADDIE GRAVES MYSTERY BOOK ONE

LILY HARPER HART

HARPERHART PUBLICATIONS

Created with Vellum

PROLOGUE

TEN YEARS AGO

"What are you doing, Maddie?"

Nick Winters rolled from his back to his side and smiled as he saw a flurry of pale blonde hair whip around in the moonlight. There she was. Maddie Graves. His best friend. His confidant. The torment of his very soul. She was the center of his world – and she was leaving. This was their last night together.

Maddie rounded off another cartwheel and landed heavily on her bare feet. Her long blonde hair was wild from the tumbling, but her blue eyes were sparkling when they focused on Nick. "Did you say something?"

They were hanging out in the open field by Willow Lake, one of the many bodies of water that surrounded Blackstone Bay on the northwestern side of Michigan's lower peninsula. It was the last night of summer, and Maddie was leaving for college the next day.

Nick raised a dark eyebrow as he regarded her. "I asked what you were doing."

"I'm playing," Maddie said, pressing her naturally pink lips together and pushing them out into an adorable pout. Even without a stitch of makeup, she was still the most beautiful thing Nick had ever seen. She didn't see it, of course, but everyone else did – including him. "This is the last time we'll be out here. I'm doing what we always do out here."

Her admission jolted him. He'd told himself a hundred times that Maddie was leaving town, but he kept hoping she would change her mind. He knew it was selfish. She had to leave Blackstone Bay to go to college. She had dreams that were bigger than one small town could yield, and yet part of him – a really selfish part – wanted her to stay. No, he needed her to stay.

"I thought you were here to spend time with me," Nick teased, tamping his misgivings down. He didn't want to ruin their last moments together.

Maddie made a face, but she ceased her endless tumbling and trudged over to the blanket he was reclining on. She took the open spot next to him, her warmth invading the previous void, and leaned her head against his shoulder. "Look how pretty it is here."

Nick and Maddie had been best friends for as long as either one of them could remember. Blackstone Bay didn't boast many options, so when you found someone who shared your interests, you had to hold on to them – even if it was someone of the opposite sex. The duo had taken a lot of guff over the years – people casting aspersions on the closeness of their relationship – but they'd never been anything more than friends.

By the time Nick realized that Maddie wasn't the gawky girl with glasses and braces anymore, they were entering their senior year of high school. Ever since then, Nick had been struggling with a new set of feelings. He just couldn't tell Maddie about them. He was sure she didn't feel the same way, and he'd rather have her as a friend than not have her at all.

Now he was facing goodbye anyway, and his heart was thudding with regret. What would happen if he told her? What would've happened if he'd admitted he loved her? What would've happened if he gave in to more than a hundred different urges and kissed her?

It was too late now.

Nick swallowed hard. "It is beautiful." He wasn't looking at the sky, instead studying the lines of her face as it rested on his chest. Maddie didn't notice.

"I'm going to miss this place," Maddie admitted.

"Then don't go." His voice was plaintive, and he forced it to remain even, but he was deadly serious.

"I have to go, Nicky," Maddie said. "The tuition has already been paid."

"And you want to go," Nick finished for her.

"Part of me does," Maddie said. "Part of me wants to stay here forever ... with you." She tapped his square chin and giggled. "Admit it. You're going to miss me."

"I *am* going to miss you," Nick said, his heart rolling painfully.

"You're only going to be here two days without me. Then you're leaving for the police academy. I'm sure you can find something to do. I know Marla Proctor has been sniffing around."

Nick wrinkled his nose. "I wouldn't touch Marla Proctor with your ten-foot pole."

Maddie snorted. "That's probably smart. I hear she's a witch. If you touch her, your ... thing will probably shrivel up and fall off."

Nick smirked. "My thing?"

Maddie ignored him – like she often did when the conversation took an odd sexual turn. "What are you going to miss most about me?"

Everything. Nick shrugged. "Nights like this. Just the two of us – and the stars."

At that exact moment, one of the stars in question streaked across the sky.

"Look," Maddie said, pointing. "It's a shooting star."

"I see it."

"Make a wish."

Nick frowned. They hadn't played this game in a long time. When they were both younger, outcasts, they used to lay on their backs in this very field and wish on every star they saw. They wished for wealth, popularity, and fame. Now, Nick only had one wish, and there was no way it was going to come true.

"You saw it first," he said. "It's yours to wish on."

Maddie's eyes momentarily flashed sadness as they focused on him. "Let's make a wish together."

Nick nodded, swallowing hard. "Okay."

They both pressed their eyelids together and lifted their chins to the stars. Nick had no idea what Maddie wished for, but his heart grabbed on to the moment and hoped for a united forever.

He didn't get his wish – at least not then. The future was yet to be written.

1. ONE

PRESENT DAY

"This is not my fault!"

"Of course it's your fault. It's always your fault."

"No, it's your fault. You pulled out in front of me."

"I didn't pull out in front of you, you old biddy. You purposely ran into me."

"Who are you calling a biddy?"

Nick Winters squeezed his eyes shut to block out the raised voices. Who knew two senior citizens could make so much noise? Given the women yelling at each other, though, he shouldn't have been surprised.

Maude Graves and Harriet Proctor had been going at each other for as long as Nick could remember. He'd spent twenty-eight years in Blackstone Bay – minus the two at the police academy down the Lake Michigan coast in Traverse City – and Maude and Harriet had been trying to yank each other's hair out all of that time. If local legend was to be believed, they'd been at it a lot longer than that.

He held up his hands to silence them. "Ladies … ."

"I want to file a complaint," Harriet said, placing her hands on her hips as she swiveled to face Nick. "She tried to murder me. I want her arrested on attempted murder charges."

"I want her arrested," Maude countered, her steel-gray curls bouncing underneath the mid-afternoon sun.

"On what charge?" Nick asked, his tone dry.

"Annoying me."

"That's not a crime," Nick pointed out.

"It is in my world."

Nick sighed. He'd known Maude his whole life. Actually, he'd known both women his whole life. He just had a soft spot for Maude. Unfortunately, he was fairly sure the accident was her fault. She shouldn't be driving as it is. Neither of them should be. Both of them were hard of hearing, and their eyesight was going. Since Blackstone Bay was such a small town, though, Nick knew better than going up against either formidable force. They could make his life miserable – even more miserable than it was right now.

"I'm not going to issue tickets," he said.

Harriet's mouth dropped open, the mole on her upper lip wrinkling as disbelief washed over her face. "Excuse me?"

Nick reined in the words that were threatening to gallop out of his mouth. "All the witnesses are telling me different things."

Harriet narrowed her eyes. "Well, if someone says it was my fault, they're lying."

"Nettie Wilder says that you pulled out in front of Maude," Nick said. He held up his hand to cut off what he was sure was about to be a nasty retort. "Evelyn Dilfer says that Maude sped up when she saw it was you. Mike Forest says that you both pulled out at the same time. Oh, and Fred Givens says a unicorn ran out in front of you and caused you to slam on your brakes so you'd entrap Maude into hitting you."

Harriet rolled her eyes. "Fred Givens should be locked up in a home."

Nick couldn't argue with that assessment. "He has some ... issues."

"Issues? That man is stoned on the marijuana every chance he gets."

Nick fought the mad urge to laugh. Fred was a notorious pot proponent, even running for governor every four years on a "free your mind" campaign. The man was in his sixties, but he didn't bother to hide his activities from anyone – including law enforcement. Since he mostly kept to himself, everyone looked the other way when he was breaking the law. He was harmless.

"We all know those aren't weeds on the back edge of his property," Harriet said.

"Some of them are weeds," Nick said. He only knew that because he'd actually pinched the weeds instead of the pot when he was in high school. That was before he became an upstanding member of the Blackstone Bay police force, of course.

"And some of them aren't."

Nick sighed. "I can either write you both tickets or I can write no one a ticket. It's up to you."

Harriet pursed her lips, and Nick could see she was shifting her dentures around the inside of her mouth as she considered her options. He slid his gaze to Maude to see how she felt about the situation. "What are your feelings, Maude?"

"I think she should be arrested and beaten to death for being a scourge on the population of this town," Maude said. "Or someone could just kick her."

She always did have a way with words.

"You heard her, she just threatened me," Harriet said. "She needs to be locked up. The people of this town aren't safe with her on the loose."

"I didn't threaten to beat you to death," Maude said.

Nick raised an eyebrow.

"I said someone else should do it," Maude clarified. "You know I have a bad hip."

"Well, that's better," Nick said, running a hand through his dark hair as his gaze bounced between the two women. The accident had been minor. The dent in Harriet's back bumper was miniscule, and Maude's front bumper was so scarred there was no way to tell what was a new dent and what was an old one. He had no idea why he was still here – or how large the interested crowd would be by the time he wrapped things up.

When he'd decided to become a police officer, Nick had visions of high-speed car chases and fleeing criminals dancing through his head. Instead of taking a chance and moving south so he could pursue more exciting opportunities, he'd opted to return to the familiar confines of Blackstone Bay. It made his mother happy, but his heart was still unsettled. He figured, one day, things would just fall into place for him. He was only twenty-eight, after all. He had plenty of time for that to happen.

"You can't just let her get away with this," Harriet said, her strawberry-colored hair bouncing as she shook her head. *Someone needs to tell her that pink is not a naturally-occurring hair hue,* Nick thought, his mind wandering. *Either she'd been lied t, or she was colorblind.* "It's not fair. It's not right."

Nick let loose with an exasperated sigh. "Harriet … ."

"Oh, shut your trap," Maude said, tapping her combat boot on the ground irritably as she shifted her floral dress around her bony body. "Stop trying to browbeat the boy. He's doing his job to the best of his ability."

"He's trying to protect you," Harriet countered. "He always takes your side."

"That's because I'm right."

"You're not right," Harriet said. "You're senile."

"You're senile."

"You're … incontinent."

Maude's drawn-on eyebrows practically flew off her forehead. "Well, I hear you wear an adult diaper."

Harriet's mouth dropped open. "I heard you pee in your drawers every time you laugh."

Maude extended a gnarled finger. "That's not incontinence," she said. "That's age. My kidneys don't work like they should. Everyone knows how that works."

"I don't have that problem," Harriet shot back.

"That's because you never laugh," Maude said. "You just cackle. That's what witches do, right? They cackle." She turned to Nick expectantly. "You heard she's a witch, right? She probably cast a spell to make me run into her."

Nick was losing track of the conversation, and his interest had long since waned. Since two sets of eyes were resting on him, though, he had a feeling he was supposed to say something. "So, where did we settle on the ticket decision?"

"I want her arrested," Harriet screeched. "She's a menace to society."

"Well, at least I don't have the herpes," Maude said.

"I don't have the herpes," Harried replied. "You stop making up things, Maude Graves."

"Lydia Donner says she saw you buying Campho-Phenique at the drug store the other day," Maude charged. "Are you calling Lydia a liar?"

Since Lydia was the favorite aunt of Blackstone Bay's esteemed mayor, it was never a wise decision to say anything untoward about the woman. She had a multitude of ears ready to report back to her if need be.

"That's because I had a cold sore," Harriet said, visibly blanching. "I'm not calling Lydia a liar." She tapped Nick's notebook. "Write that down."

"That's the herpes," Maude said, pointing at Harriet's lip.

"It's a cold sore."

"Caused by the herpes."

"You're a herpes," Harriet said.

"No, you're a herpes."

Nick would've welcome actual herpes if it would get him out of this conversation. "Ladies … ."

"I want *her* taken to jail," Harriet said.

"No," Nick said.

"I want *her* taken to jail," Maude said.

"No."

"I want … ."

"No more," Nick said, raising his hands in the air testily. "Either you're both going to jail, or everyone is going to agree this was just an accident and move on." If he could just end this here, his shift would be over. He could go home and drown his sorrows in a bottle of bourbon and some much-welcomed silence. That sounded heavenly right about now.

"Maybe *you* should be put in jail, Nick," Harriet suggested.

"For what?"

"Elder abuse," Harriet said. "What? That's a real thing."

Elder abuse sounded like a pretty good solution. Nick pinched the bridge of his nose. "Listen … ."

"Granny?"

Nick froze when he heard the voice. He would've recognized it anywhere, even though it had been a decade since he heard it. His body was rigid as he turned, his dark eyes falling on the face that still haunted his dreams as it emerged from the crowd of interested onlookers. "Maddie?"

2. TWO

Maddie Graves felt as if someone had run over her with a truck. One look at Nick – the familiar dark eyes and strong chin from a decade before harkening back to better times – and her world came crashing down.

She knew he was still in town. Maude kept her updated on his comings and goings – even though she didn't want to hear them. Memories of Nick were just too painful. She knew what she'd lost when she said goodbye to him. She didn't need constant reminders.

"Nick." His name came out as a strangled gasp. She sucked in a breath and gathered herself together. "Nick," she repeated, this time calmer.

Nick's face had gone from conflicted to haunted the moment he laid eyes on her. She registered the shock as it washed across the angular planes of his face. She hadn't seen him in ten years, and yet it felt like just yesterday they'd been wishing on stars in a field and fighting for every second they had together before real life tore them apart.

"Maddie." Nick took a tentative step toward her. "What are you doing here?"

Maddie closed the gap between them, her knees shaking with every step. "I just got back."

Nick opened his arms and pulled her in for an awkward hug. Maddie melted into him for a second, her body reacting to the familiarity of his scent – he still smelled like the woods they used to frolic in – and her face fit into the hollow between his neck and chest as he held her. *Home*, she thought briefly.

After a moment, Nick pulled away so he could look her up and down. "You look … ."

"Older?" Maddie supplied, a small smile playing across her lips.

"I was going to say the same," Nick replied, his chocolate brown eyes conflicted. "You haven't changed a bit."

Maddie didn't believe that for a second. "You have."

Nick furrowed his brow.

"You're taller," Maddie said, smiling. "You were always tall, but you're really tall now." He was also more muscular. Maddie had no doubt the body that resided under his cute little uniform was something to behold. She always knew he would grow into his looks, but she had no idea the outcome would be this … breathtaking.

Nick swallowed. "So, are you just here for a visit?"

Maddie shook her head. She'd imagined this conversation so many different times, she was genuinely curious where it would actually go. "I'm back to stay."

"W-w-what?" The word was barely a whisper.

"I'm here to stay," Maddie said, biting her bottom lip to calm her nerves. "Someone needs to take care of Granny."

"I don't need someone to take care of me," Maude argued. "And I told you not to call me that. I don't want anyone to know I'm old enough to be a grandmother."

Nick's eyes flashed with amusement. "No one would ever believe you're old enough to be a grandmother, Maude."

"Only people with eyes," Harriet said.

"You shut your herpes-infested mouth," Maude shot back.

Nick glanced over his shoulder reluctantly. Things were going to get out of hand again if he wasn't careful. Maddie's sudden reappearance was more pressing than Harriet and Maude's fight, though. "I was sorry to hear about Olivia."

Maddie swallowed hard. Her mother's death had been weighing on her since she'd received the devastating call a month before. She hadn't been sick. She hadn't been tired. She hadn't been anything but full of light. Still, the knowledge that Olivia had died alone in her bed – an undetected heart problem stalking her for years – had thrown Maddie. It had taken weeks of looking over her options – and her life – to make Maddie realize that her only choice was to return home. "Thank you."

"There was no funeral," Nick said.

"She didn't like them," Maddie said. "She didn't want people to look at her while she was dead, and she didn't want a bunch of people crying over her after she'd moved on."

"That sounds like her," Nick said.

"Yeah," Maddie said, shifting uncomfortably. "She was cremated. I'm going to spread her ashes out at Willow Lake when I get settled. It's what she wanted."

"She always loved the lake."

"She wasn't the only one," Maddie pointed out.

"So, you're just ... coming home to take care of Maude?"

"I don't need anyone to take care of me," Maude protested.

"Yes, you do," Maddie said, rolling her eyes as she turned back to Nick. "I'm also going to be taking over Magicks." Magicks was her mother's store. It was a hodgepodge of candles, herbs, tarot card readings, and other kitschy items, and it was a mainstay in Blackstone Bay. Maddie couldn't bear to let it go, and Maude was incapable of running it without her.

"You're giving up being a nurse?" Nick seemed surprised.

"I haven't been a nurse in a few years," Maddie admitted.

"Why not? That's what you went to college for. That's why you ... left."

Maddie shrugged. That was a conversation for another time – one where they didn't have an audience. "It's a long story."

Nick nodded. "I didn't think ... you said you'd never come back."

"I was wrong," Maddie said simply.

Nick cocked his head to the side as Maude and Harriet started going at each other again behind him. "I … ."

"I know," Maddie said, her heart pinging. "Hey, I'm home for good now. I'm sure we can … catch up … soon."

"Right," Nick said, his voice flat. "We'll just … catch up."

"WELL, that didn't go very well."

Maddie glanced over at Maude, who was sitting in the passenger seat of her car as Maddie navigated the side streets of Blackstone Bay and headed to the outskirts of town. "What didn't go very well?"

"Your big reunion with Nick."

"What big reunion?"

"You two used to be closer than a virgin's thighs at a whorehouse," Maude said. "What I saw today was downright pitiful."

"First of all, that's a really odd – and obnoxious – saying," Maddie said. "Second of all, what was pitiful? We haven't seen each other in forever. It's not like we're still in high school."

"He's your best friend."

"He *was* my best friend," Maddie corrected. "Time changes things."

"Yeah, that's why your face is paler than Santa Claus' butt hair."

"Stop saying things like that," Maddie snapped. "You just do it for attention. You know it, and I know it."

"Don't change the subject," Maude said. "I want to know what you're feeling."

"I'm not feeling anything."

"Oh, Madeline Graves, don't run that on me," Maude said. "I know how you felt about that boy."

Maddie refused to look at her grandmother. She was afraid, if she did, the woman would see all of the emotions she was busily trying to tamp down. "He was my best friend."

"You loved him," Maude said. "You always loved him. First, you loved him as the boy you went frogging with in the summer. Then you loved him as the boy you went mushroom hunting with in the spring. Then you loved him as the boy who had all the girls chasing him in middle school. Then you really loved him as the boy who broke hearts all across town in high school. He was more than your best friend."

Maddie sighed. She hated Maude's insight. The woman had always been a wonderful grandmother – taking her on adventures as a child, serving as a sounding board when her mother didn't have time to listen to her problems as a teenager – but she had an eerie way of being able to look into Maddie's soul. It made her uncomfortable. "I loved him as my best friend."

"Maddie," Maude snorted, exasperated. "You might have been able to convince yourself of that while you were away, but you're not going to be able to keep up that charade now that you're back. You two won't be able to stay away from each other."

"We're adults now," Maddie said. "A lot has changed."

"And some things never change," Maude said. "Some things ... some things are just forever, Maddie. You and Nick are forever."

Part of Maddie wanted to believe that. The other part was more realistic. "We haven't talked to each other in a decade."

"And whose fault is that?" Maude challenged.

"Well, it's certainly not mine," Maddie said.

"Really? He called you all the time after you left for college," Maude said. "You dodged his calls until he gave up."

That was only partially true, but Maddie was feeling belligerent. "Our lives went in different directions."

"Because you picked a direction he couldn't follow," Maude said. "Hell, girl, you picked a direction you couldn't stick to either."

"What are you talking about?"

"Don't even deny it," Maude said. "I know why you chose to go to college down south. I know what was weighing on you when you did it, and I understand having to get away. You didn't have to choose to live there, though. You could've come home when you graduated. You could've had that boy then."

Maddie made a face as she turned into the driveway in front of Magicks. The store was located on the main floor of an old Victorian, one that Maude and her late husband, Homer, had purchased and renovated fifty years before. Now, the family lived on the second floor of the home and ran the business out of the main floor. "I could never have Nick." She killed the engine of Maude's car and handed the keys over to her grandmother. "He never was … mine."

"Oh, Maddie, you're so blind you need to find those big glasses you used to wear in middle school," Maude said. "You know the ones that made you look like a constipated tortoise? You clearly need them."

"Granny … ."

"Don't call me that," Maude warned, wagging a finger in Maddie's direction. "Girl, just listen to me for a second. I know you never thought that Nick noticed you in that way. And it's true, it took him a long time to recognize what was in front of him, but you crushed him when you left. You broke his heart. He was a sad and depressed mess."

"He let me go."

"What choice did he have, Maddie? Should he have stalked you to Ann Arbor? Should he have wrestled you down and made you see the light? You chose to leave."

"And he chose to stay."

"And now you chose to come home," Maude said. "You can say it's to take care of me, and if you keep telling people that, by the way, I'm going to thump you good." Maude waved her clenched fist in Maddie's face. "You didn't just come home because of me, though. You didn't just come home because of the store. You came home because of him, too."

"He's got a life that doesn't include me, Granny," Maddie said, purposely using the one word she knew continuously drove Maude over the deep end. "I came home to build a new life."

"And you don't think Nick will be part of that life?"

"I think there's too much water under that bridge," Maddie said, pushing open the car door. "Come on. You can cook dinner while I start getting the store in order. It's a mess down there."

"You're a piece of work, Maddie girl," Maude said. "You always did have to go about things the hard way. It's darned unfortunate."

"Everything is going to work out, Granny," she said. "It's going to be fine."

"It *is* going to be fine," Maude agreed, following Maddie up the front steps. "You just don't realize how fine it's going to be because you're downright stubborn. You'll find out, though, and I don't think it will take very long."

"Go cook dinner," Maddie said, exasperated.

"Fine," Maude said. "I hope you like casserole."

"I love casserole," Maddie said.

"Well, mine tastes like feet," Maude said. "You'll live, though. We all know you're too pretty to cook."

Maddie watched her grandmother make her way through the store and disappear inside the bowels of the house. Once she was gone, she let the emotions nudging at the edges of her heart take over. Seeing Nick had been harder than she imagined. Her initial reaction to him had been purely physical. When he'd wrapped his arms around her, she'd wanted to climb inside of him. The gesture was friendly and strained, but there had been nothing on his part to indicate familiarity. It was just two old acquaintances doing what was expected of them.

That probably hurt more than anything else. She'd expected him to do something. Yell. Rant. Rave. Scream. Shake her. *Something.* Something that would indicate he still cared. None of that was present.

"Well, I guess it's better this way," Maddie muttered, reaching over to a nearby shelf and grabbing a box.

"What's better this way?"

Maddie yelped at the voice, inadvertently stumbling backward as a familiar figure blinked into view. "Hello, Mother."

3. THREE

"You don't look happy, sunshine."

Maddie drew in a deep breath and steadied her nerves as she took in her mother's filmy countenance. She'd expected this. That was another reason she'd returned home. If she couldn't have her mother in life, she wanted her in death. She fought the urge to cry when her mother's ghost used the familiar nickname of a happy childhood. "Mom."

"I wish I could give you a hug," Olivia said, tilting her head to the side. "You look like you need one."

Maddie pressed her eyes together briefly, and then wrenched them open so she could study the familiar lines of her mother's face. Olivia Graves had aged well, which meant she'd retained her beauty in death. She'd lived a clean life. No smoking. No alcohol. Even though her husband had left her when Maddie was a baby, and Olivia had been relegated to long hours of work for meager pay, the woman never gave in to the hardships of life.

"I've missed you," Maddie said, her eyes filling with tears. "I knew you would be here."

"I could never leave you," Olivia said.

"What about Granny?"

"Her either," Olivia said, smiling. "I saw you two come back together. You were arguing. Did something happen?"

"She rear-ended Harriet Proctor."

Olivia nodded knowingly. "Did they insult each other?"

"According to Granny, Harriet has the herpes," Maddie said, smiling. She'd missed talking to her mother. It would never be the same. They'd never be able to touch each other again. Maddie would never be able to curl up on her mother's lap and tell her a lifetime's worth of woes, but Maddie's "peculiarity" was a gift – in this case, at least.

"Well, I'm glad she's feeling better," Olivia said. "It's been hard to watch her struggle since my ... passing."

Maddie had been able to see ghosts since she was a small child. The first time it happened, she'd been traumatized. She'd raced home to tell her mother what the man in the strange uniform told her at the cemetery. After five cups of hot cocoa – and a multitude of mini-marshmallows – Olivia had laid out a lifetime legacy to Maddie. The "peculiarity" ran in the family. Maude didn't have it, but her mother and sister had. Olivia had, too, so she wasn't surprised when her daughter manifested the ability.

Now? Now it was a blessing. "She doesn't know you're here?"

"You know she can't see the dead, sunshine," Olivia said. "She always felt lucky because it skipped her."

"I'm betting she doesn't feel so lucky now," Maddie said, settling on the chair behind the counter, her mind busy. "Mom ... ?"

"I didn't know what was happening," Olivia said, reading the emotion on her daughter's face. "I was asleep. I didn't feel it. There was no pain. There was no fear."

"How did you know what I was thinking?"

"That's what a mother does," Olivia said, raising her ethereal hand and miming running it over Maddie's hair. "You look beautiful."

"I look like I've always looked," Maddie scoffed. "I'm just boring, old Maddie."

"Oh, sweetie, you've never been able to see yourself," Olivia said. "I blame myself. I didn't build up your self-esteem enough as a child."

"Wasn't that Granny's job?"

"And she was good at it," Olivia said. "It still would've been better coming from me."

"You were a great mother," Maddie argued. "You gave me everything I ever needed."

"Except a smile," Olivia said, studying Maddie's face. "What were you and Mom arguing about when you came in?"

Maddie wrinkled her nose. "She's convinced I handled things badly with Nick this afternoon."

Olivia was interested, her blues eyes widening at Maddie's admission. "You saw Nick today?"

"He was called to the scene of the accident."

"Poor, Nick," Olivia said, chuckling. "He's got the patience of a saint, and he needs it with those two going at each other."

"He looked like he was ready to throttle them both."

"And how did he react to seeing you?" Olivia's question was pointed.

Maddie averted her gaze. "He seemed surprised."

"And?"

"He gave me a quick hug, and then we had to go."

Olivia's face was hard to read. "I'm betting there was more to it than that."

Maddie plastered an inscrutable look on her face. "Why are you and Granny so convinced there's some conspiracy about my relationship with Nick? We were friends – a lifetime ago – and now we're just old acquaintances."

"Is that what you're telling yourself these days?" Olivia asked.

"It's the truth."

Olivia's enigmatic smile set Maddie's teeth on edge. "Keep telling yourself that, sunshine. The longer you keep deluding yourself, the longer you'll be in pain."

"What is that supposed to mean?"

"You know exactly what it means," Olivia chided. "Don't act stupid. You're a bright girl, Maddie Graves. I've always known that. The only thing you can't see is the truth when it comes to Nick – and yourself. You're clearly not ready to see what's in front of you, so I'm not going to push you. How about, instead, we get the store organized? It seems to have fallen into disarray during my death."

"Granny has interesting cleaning habits," Maddie agreed.

"Since I can't help, I'll supervise," Olivia offered, smiling widely. "I think this is going to be fun."

NICK PUMPED his legs hard as he climbed the hill, raising his knees high as he finished the fifth mile of his morning run. His mind was busy, memories of his past colliding with the uncertainty of his future as he tried to wrap his brain around Maddie's sudden arrival the day before.

What was she doing back here?

There had been a time when Nick had been convinced he would marry Maddie. He knew it in the fiber of his very being. He had grand delusions of her triumphant return to Blackstone Bay after getting her nursing degree, of her racing into his arms and admitting she loved him the second she crossed the town line. He saw a big wedding, children, and happily ever after.

Those fantasies had all been for naught.

It had taken years for Nick to finally relinquish them. When she left for college, Nick considered going after her. He even had his truck packed and a speech written down on a napkin to recite back to her, one that professed his love in no uncertain terms. His courage failed that day. *What would've happened if it hadn't?*

For the first few months, Nick called her every week. She answered eagerly at first. He could almost hear her fighting off tears over the phone as they talked. After a few weeks, though, she stopped answering his calls. It had taken months for him to give up, each unanswered call poking another hole in his heart. He was bitter after a time, and he'd spent years cursing her very existence – mostly because her angelic face kept haunting his dreams.

Now? Now he was thrown. Every hateful thing he'd ever thought about Maddie flew out of his mind – and memory – the second he saw her. He'd hugged her out of instinct, and the way she'd melted into his arms caused a familiar longing to bubble back up.

Dammit! He was still in love with her. After ten years, after a multitude of nightmares and despondent tears, after ... everything ... he was still in love with her. He was a glutton for punishment. There could be no other explanation.

Maddie had seemed so ... distant ... when she approached him. She'd always been shy, but the woman standing in front of him the day before had seemed haunted more than anything else. He didn't like it.

A flash of flaxen hair caught Nick's attention out of the corner of his eye. He jerked his head, his heart skipping a beat when he recognized Maddie's long blonde hair as it flopped in the wind. He knew it was her without hesitation. Her hair was in a ponytail, and her lithe body was in a pair of jogging shorts and a tight tank top – one of those ones with a bra built in, so his imagination didn't have to wander too far – but he knew it was her without even giving it a second thought.

He didn't care, Nick told himself. She hadn't cared enough to keep in contact with him, and he certainly didn't care about her return. She was nothing but an old friend. Despite himself, Nick found his pace increasing.

When he crested the hill that overlooked Willow Lake, he almost crashed into her. She was standing, her fingers pressed to her neck as she checked her pulse, and she was oblivious to his presence. Her sea-blue eyes widened as he zoomed into view. She pulled to the side to avoid the imminent collision, and the change in his trajectory caused him to lose his footing and topple to the side.

"Holy crap!"

"I ... ." Nick looked up at her from the ground, rubbing his knee ruefully as he regarded her. "What are you doing?"

"What are you doing?"

"I was out for my morning run," Nick said, fighting to catch his breath. He wanted to believe he was gasping because of his workout, but he knew that wasn't entirely true. She'd knocked the air out of him, like she always did. "What are you doing?"

Maddie gestured to her tiny outfit. "The same thing you are." She extended her hand to help him up.

Nick took the proffered hand begrudgingly, and when he was back on his feet, he looked her body over with the studied eyes of a trained police officer. She'd had a fantastic body as a teenager, but age had only done favorable things to it. Her legs were long and toned, her midriff tight. And her breasts? He'd give anything to see what was under that tank top. Anything.

"I didn't know you liked to run," Nick said after a beat.

"Well, I like to eat," Maddie said. "That means I have to run."

Nick pursed his lips. "I guess that makes sense."

Maddie rubbed a hand over her forehead, brushing the accumulated sweat from her brow. Her face was devoid of makeup, and just like when she was a teenager, Nick couldn't imagine anyone ever accumulating enough beauty to touch her.

"You look good, Nick."

He was surprised by the compliment. "You look good, too."

"So, um, how have you been?"

Nick snorted. "Really? That's your opening line?"

"I'm not sure what you mean," Maddie said, rubbing her hands over her midriff self-consciously.

"You know, Maddie, I've been imagining what I would say to you – if I ever saw you again, that is – for ten years now," Nick said.

"And how is that going?"

"Not good," Nick said. "I had a lot of mean things stored up where you were concerned."

Maddie's face fell. "I … ."

"No, it's my turn now," Nick said. "You just cut me out of your life, Maddie. You pretended I didn't exist."

"I got … I had a lot going on," Maddie said lamely.

"We both had a lot going on, Mad," he said, shortening her name like he'd so often done during their childhood. "I still managed to pick up a phone."

"You don't understand, Nicky," Maddie said.

Nick's heart rolled painfully when she used the nickname only she'd ever been allowed to utter. "What don't I understand?"

"Life was always so easy for you," Maddie said, her eyes flooding with tears. "Sure, we were both losers in elementary school, but when we got to middle school, everyone suddenly noticed you. I was just the geek you deigned to spend time with.

"Even in high school, I could see the way all those girls looked at me," she continued. "You were the big stud on campus. You were the quarterback, and point guard, and ... whatever it was you did on the track team. I was just the ugly girl at your side, and no one could understand why you were friends with me."

Nick was incredulous. "Ugly?"

"You saw how they looked at me, Nicky," Maddie charged on. "I was your ... charity case."

"I never felt that way," Nick said, anger coursing through him.

"I know you didn't," Maddie said, softening. "It was different for me when I got away, though. I wasn't the daughter of a single mother who had to walk around in used clothes anymore. I didn't have people snickering behind my back. I wasn't exactly popular at college, but I could hide there. No one noticed me, and I was happy not to be noticed. I wasn't anyone's charity case."

Nick was having trouble believing no one at college had ever noticed her. "Really? No one noticed you?"

"Oh, sure, frat boys," Maddie said, her tone dismissive. "They were always trying to get me into bed, but it was only because they'd nail anything with a pulse."

Nick scowled. "Sleep with a lot of frat boys, did you?"

Maddie's face was murderous. "No. I'm not into being used for sex and then dumped."

Nick was at a loss. She either had no idea what she looked like or she was putting on a show for his benefit. His battered heart decided it had to be the latter. "I don't know what you want me to say, Mad. You seem to want to make me the villain in all of this. I was the one left behind." He pounded his chest. "I was the one ignored. I was the one forgotten."

"Nicky ... ."

"Don't," he warned. "I can't even look at you. You're so not the person I thought you were."

It took every effort he had, but Nick turned away from Maddie and her crumbling face. He jogged away without a second look. He was done here. He was so done.

4. FOUR

Maddie stopped outside Cuts & Curls, the local beauty parlor, and sucked in a breath. She never thought she'd be here again. She knew the local parlor was gossip central for Blackstone Bay, but she desperately needed a trim. Her hair was raggedy, and six months of neglect was making her feel self-conscious. Since the town only had one parlor, she had two options: Suck it up, or drive forty miles out of her way. She was tired of running from this town – and its denizens.

When she entered Cuts & Curls, she wasn't surprised to see the same fading wallpaper and vinyl chairs. There's comfort in simplicity, and Cuts & Curls wasn't trying to be fancy.

Maddie walked up to the front counter, refusing to scan the various women in the shop (even though she could feel their eyes boring into her), and waited. Finally, a woman with flame-red hair piled on top of her head – messy curls spilling out in every direction – bounced up to the counter. "Can I help you?"

"Um, yeah, I just need a trim," Maddie said. "I don't have an appointment, but I'm willing to wait. It shouldn't take more than a few minutes. I don't need a wash or anything."

The woman across the counter studied Maddie for a moment, and then her face broke into a wide grin. "Maddie Graves?"

Maddie faltered. "Yeah."

"It's me," the woman said, patting her ample chest. "Christy Ford."

Memories swirled in Maddie's head. Christy Ford? The only Christy Ford she could remember had been a rotund girl with a bright smile and an infectious laugh. Maddie didn't have a lot of friends in high school, Nick notwithstanding, but Christy had been an ally in a sea of mean girls. "Christy?" Maddie studied her more intently. The girl she remembered had been blessed with a round face, emerald green eyes, and bland brown hair. The brown hair was gone, and the round face had narrowed some, but the green eyes were still there.

"Holy crap, girl," Christy said, bounding around the counter and enveloping Maddie in an invasive hug. "You look amazing!"

Maddie gasped for breath. "You do, too."

"Oh, don't lie," Christy said, smiling. "I look like a big raspberry. You, though, you could be a model."

Christy was always the first one to utter a compliment, even if it was completely untrue. "How have you been?"

"Good," Christy said, gesturing to the open spot closest to the front counter. "Come on. I can give you a trim."

Maddie settled in the chair, letting Christy cover her with a frock without complaint or further comment. Christy studied her hair for a few minutes, poking at her roots and then focusing on Maddie's face in the mirror. "Is this your natural color?"

Maddie nodded. "I know it's kind of ... flat."

"Flat? Girl, people would kill for this color. It's amazing," Christy said. She reached for the bottle of water on the counter and started spraying. "Do you want any length off?"

"Not really," Maddie said. She'd never really focused on her hair. People noticed it, so she figured it was one of her few attractive attributes. "Just cut an inch or so off the ends."

"The form is good," Christy said, running her hands down Maddie's head. "The natural highlights are gorgeous. The ends are kind of split, though."

"I haven't had it cut in six months," Maddie admitted.

"I'll have it looking great in fifteen minutes," Christy said, reaching for a pair of scissors. "So, what are you doing back in town?"

"I'm taking over my mom's store."

Christy faltered. "I was really sorry to hear about Olivia," she said. "I always liked her. She read my cards once a month. She always told me great things."

Maddie's mom told everyone great things. If she saw any hardship in the cards, which she was capable of doing (that was part of the "peculiarity"), she always left it out. People don't want to hear bad things. That's what she'd always told Maddie anyway.

"She was a good woman," Maddie said, fighting to keep her voice even.

"She was," Christy said, happily snipping at the ends of Maddie's hair. "So, have you seen Nick?"

Maddie shifted uncomfortably. "Yeah. Why?"

"I just always thought you two were a couple," Christy said. "It didn't occur to me that you weren't until you left him high and dry and went to college."

"That's not really what happened," Maddie mumbled.

"It's none of my business," Christy said. "So, how does it feel to be back?"

"Weird," Maddie admitted. "Nothing has changed, and yet it feels like everything has changed."

"Because of your mom?" Christy was sage. Maddie had forgotten that. She had a natural ability to read people.

"I miss her."

"Of course you do," Christy said, her eyes narrowing sympathetically. "She was the only family you had."

"I have Granny."

"You do have her," Christy agreed, laughing. "She comes in once a month. She was suspicious for six months after I bought the place, but now she lets me set her hair without threatening to set my house on fire."

"Oh, you bought the salon?" Maddie was surprised. "Granny never told me that."

"Well, I always did love this place," Christy said. "I never had wandering thoughts, so I never wanted to leave. When I decided what I wanted to do with my life, this was what I pictured. So I went to that beauticians' school over in Traverse City, and then I came back here.

"I worked here for five years, and then when Louise wanted to retire, she agreed to sell it to me," she continued. "I've been the owner for three years now. I love it."

Maddie admired her. She knew what she wanted, and she'd gone after it. Her aims weren't high. She knew what would make her happy, though. Maddie had never known what would make her happy. She'd followed the dream she thought she was supposed to, and been miserable the whole time.

"So, what are you doing for fun since you came back?" Christy asked, oblivious to the heavy thoughts plundering Maddie's mind.

"Well, I had to pick Granny up after she rear-ended Harriet yesterday."

Christy barked out a laugh. "I heard about that. It was quite the town gossip."

"It certainly was."

Maddie froze when she heard the voice. She recognized it ... from her nightmares. "Marla Proctor," Maddie said, keeping her voice even.

"Maddie Graves." Marla's face appeared in the mirror behind Christy.

She still looked the same, Maddie mused. Her dark hair was long and flat. There was no "bounce" to it. There never had been. Marla's features were narrow and pleasing – if you liked the "ferret" look. She'd been popular in high school, nabbing every boy she'd ever set her sights on – except for Nick. That had been the major bone of contention between Marla and Maddie, from their middle-school years onward. Nick Winters was the prize, and Marla just couldn't claim him.

"How are you?" Maddie asked, refusing to lower herself to a dirty argument.

"I'm great," Marla said. "Well, I was great until I heard you came back to town."

"Marla, I won't take any of your nonsense," Christy warned. "Maddie is a paying customer here."

"I pay you every week when I come in," Marla countered.

"And, as long as you don't attack any of my other clients, you're welcome," Christy said. "That doesn't mean I like you."

Maddie stilled. She wasn't the only person Marla had terrorized in high school. She'd almost forgotten. Christy had been another victim of the malicious guttersnipe.

"Now, Christy, you know I've apologized for any ... misunderstandings ... in high school," Marla soothed.

"You call them misunderstandings," Christy countered. "I remember the actual events."

"But ... ."

Christy raised the scissors in warning. "Don't push me, Marla. I will ban you."

"Oh, so you're taking 'Greasy Graves' side?"

Maddie's stomach twisted. That had been her slur in high school. Marla was one of those girls who got off on making others feel like dirt. Some things never change.

"Okay," Christy said, her tone clipped. "You can leave now. You don't have to pay your bill, but you're done."

Marla's hands raised to her hair, her face mutinous. "I haven't gotten my set yet. I have a date tonight."

"You should have thought about that before you insulted Maddie," Christy replied, nonplussed. "I told you the rules when I took this place over. It's not my fault you can't follow them."

"You can't do this," Marla screeched. "I'm a paying customer."

"You can be a paying customer in another town," Christy said. "The money isn't worth the hassle of putting up with you."

"You listen to me, Christy Ford," Marla said, waving a finger around haphazardly. "If you toss me out of this place, I'll tell everyone to stop coming here."

"Go ahead," Christy said, not phased in the least. "I've been turning away people every week. Losing you and that little gaggle of harpies you run around with isn't going to hurt me. In fact, it will probably make this place more popular."

"You can't do this!"

"I just did," Christy said, her eyes focused on Maddie's hair. "Get out."

Marla scanned the salon for sympathetic faces. Finding none, she mustered whatever dignity she could find, gathered her purse, and then flounced out of the salon. "You'll be sorry."

"Bye," Christy said, not bothering to look up.

Once Marla left, the assembled women in the salon broke out into spontaneous applause. Maddie's face was flushed when she met Christy's eyes in the mirror. "You didn't have to do that. I could've just left."

"Oh, Maddie," Christy said, running her hands down the sides of the blonde woman's hair. "I'd much rather have you here than her. You just need to learn how to stand up for yourself. Marla Proctor is nothing more than a bully. She's always been a bully, and she'll always be a bully. There's only one way to deal with a bully."

"And what way is that?"

"You bully them right back," Christy said, smiling. "Your hair is really beautiful."

Maddie fought the urge to cry. "Thank you."

Maddie caught a hint of movement out of the corner of her eye. She stiffened involuntarily when a woman – a young one with extraordinary brown waves and expressive green eyes – approached her nervously. She was wearing a smock, which meant she'd been there to witness the verbal sparring with Marla. Maddie was on edge.

"Hey, Cassidy," Christy said, not breaking stride as she snipped the ends of Maddie's hair. "Is something wrong?"

"No," Cassidy replied, unsure.

Maddie wracked her brain. She didn't remember anyone named Cassidy from high school. The woman looked to be about the same age as she and Christy. She braced herself for a verbal onslaught.

"Are you really Maddie Graves?"

Maddie met Christy's eyes, confused. "Yes."

"I'm Cassidy Dunham," she said, extending her hand. "I just wanted to meet you. I never thought I would get to. I'm just really excited." She smoothed the smock covering her clothes. "You're a legend around here."

Maddie looked to Christy for help. Christy took pity on her. "Cassidy has been in town for about two years now," she said.

"I'm a school teacher," Cassidy supplied helpfully.

"Oh, well, great," Maddie said, confused. "It's really nice to meet you."

Christy licked her lips. "She's also Nick Winters' girlfriend."

Maddie wasn't sure, but she felt as if her heart had just exploded. "Oh, well … ."

"I know you and Nick were close in school," Cassidy said, her face guileless. "There's just this weird … hype … around Blackstone Bay where you two are concerned."

Maddie felt like she was caught in quicksand. "I'm not sure what to say to that."

"Oh, I'm making you uncomfortable," Cassidy said, running her hand over her peaches-and-cream cheek worriedly. "I'm so sorry. This is not the way I wanted to meet you."

Maddie searched Christy's face for answers. Finding none, she turned to Cassidy. "You wanted to meet me?" This was all so … surreal.

"Of course," Cassidy said. "You knew my Nick when he was a small boy. I want to know all of the stories."

"Your … Nick?" Maddie almost choked on the words.

"We've been together for six months now," Cassidy said. "He's just so … wonderful."

"He's a good guy," Maddie said, lowering her gaze.

"He tells me such fun stories," Cassidy enthused. "You're in all of them."

"We spent a lot of time together as kids," Maddie hedged.

Cassidy clapped her hands together excitedly. "I know. We should all go to lunch together."

Maddie's eyebrows flew up her forehead. "What?"

"You need to get your hair finished," Cassidy said, running her hand down the back of her own hair. "I do, too. We can't talk properly. We need to go to lunch when we're finished up here. I have so many questions I want to ask."

"I don't know … ."

"Christy will come, too, won't you?"

Christy looked caught. "I'd love to," she said, patting Maddie's shoulder in a comforting manner. "We'll all go to lunch together."

Maddie wasn't convinced. Christy fixed her with a hard look. "It will be good for you."

Maddie forced a tight smile onto her face. "It sounds … great."

"Yay!"

5. FIVE

"Oh, this is so exciting."

Maddie was having trouble finding the energy to agree with Cassidy's enthusiastic take on the situation. Instead of answering, she settled into one of the open chairs at Ruby's Diner and glanced around. "This place is exactly how I remember it."

"Yeah, there's not a lot about Blackstone Bay that changes," Christy agreed, taking the spot next to her and shifting on the vinyl chair to make herself comfortable. "It's like being caught in a time warp."

"It's almost easier," Maddie said.

"Why do you say that?"

"Because, if everything had changed, then it would be like the town moved on without me," Maddie admitted. "Wait ... that sounded really narcissistic, didn't it?"

"I think it makes sense," Christy said. "It's hard to leave home, but it's even harder to come back."

"Especially when you never thought you would," Maddie murmured, her gaze landing on the booth in the back corner of the diner. That was "her" spot. Well, technically, that was "their" spot. That's where she and Nick met every day after school to have an afternoon snack. That's the spot where they had lemonade in the summer. That's the spot … .

"So, tell me what Nick was like when you were kids."

Cassidy's voice broke Maddie out of her reverie. "Um, I don't know," she said. "He was normal. He liked to do … boy things. He liked to chase frogs and turtles down at Willow Lake and play football and basketball."

"He still does that," Cassidy said. "Go down to Willow Lake, I mean."

Maddie felt as if her tongue was lodged in her throat. "Do you go down to the lake with him?"

If Cassidy registered Maddie's discomfort, she didn't let on. "Oh, no, that's his private spot. He says that's where he likes to go and think. I'm betting it was like that when you were kids, right? Did he think down there by himself every day?"

"Um … sure," Maddie said carefully.

Christy rolled her eyes. "Oh, please, that's where you two always went together." She realized what she'd said too late, but she didn't retract the statement. "Sorry, Cassidy."

"Why are you sorry?" Cassidy's pretty face was filled with confusion.

"It's just that everyone in town knew that Willow Lake was Nick and Maddie's spot," Christy explained. "We had bets on what they were doing down there. When we were little, we figured they were drawing up their plans for world domination."

Cassidy giggled.

"When they were older, we were convinced that's where they went to do it," Christy said.

"Christy!" Maddie was mortified.

"Hey, you two spent far too much time together for nothing to be going on," Christy said. "Whenever the hottest guy and prettiest girl in school spend all of their time together, you just know something is going on. Spill."

Maddie's face was mottled with color. "There was nothing going on." She shot an apologetic look in Cassidy's direction. "Christy was always really dramatic."

"It's fine," Cassidy said, her face unreadable. "I wanted to hear the stories."

"You're saying that all of the times you and Nick went down there – the night before you left for college included – nothing happened?" Christy's eyes were narrowed with suspicion. "I don't believe you."

"How do you know we were down at the lake before I left for college?" Maddie was flabbergasted. "Did you spy on us?"

"No," Christy said, waving Maddie's accusation off with her perfectly manicured hand. "Everyone knew where you two were, Maddie. Every girl in that school had a crush on Nick – and he pretty much ignored all of them. They kept walking outside of his house to get him to notice them, but he never even acknowledged them. You were the only one he ever cared about. Even when he took Anna Lipscomb to prom, he didn't pay any attention to her."

"So, you two dated?" Cassidy asked, her voice taking on a slight edge.

"We didn't date," Maddie said. "We were just friends. Nick was not interested in me that way. Trust me. Christy just likes ... telling stories."

"And what is Christy telling stories about?"

Maddie froze when she heard Nick's voice, cool dread washing over her.

"Nick," Cassidy squealed, jumping up from the table and throwing her arms around his broad shoulders. "I didn't know you were going to be here. Look, I found Maddie. She was at the beauty parlor."

Nick smiled tightly as he awkwardly patted Cassidy's back. He was clearly uncomfortable. "I see. You met at the beauty parlor and all decided to ... go to lunch together?"

"Cassidy insisted," Christy said, attempting to deflect Nick's ire from Maddie. "She thinks Maddie is a shiny new toy to play with."

Cassidy smirked. "She does kind of look like a human Barbie doll."

Nick locked eyes with Maddie. "I guess she does."

"You should join us," Cassidy said, yanking on his hand and drawing him toward the open chair next to Maddie. "We were just talking about you guys."

"What guys?" Nick asked, worried. He took the seat anyway. Cassidy wasn't giving him much of a choice.

"You and Maddie," Cassidy said. "You were a lot closer than you let on, by the way. I'll bet that's because she's so pretty, and you didn't want me to be jealous."

"I … um … what stories have you been telling her exactly?" Nick asked, his tone accusatory.

"I didn't tell her anything," Maddie protested. "I promise."

"Maddie didn't tell me anything," Cassidy said, wrinkling her ski-slope nose in Nick's direction. "Why are you so angry?"

"If Maddie didn't tell you anything, who did?"

Christy raised her hand, blasé. "I just told her what everyone in town was thinking when we were teenagers."

"Which was?"

"Apparently everyone in town thought you and Maddie were down at Willow Lake having sex," Cassidy said, giggling. "It's weird, though. You told me that you always went to Willow Lake alone because you like to think."

Nick pursed his lips. "I … well … I do."

"But you were always there with Maddie when you were kids," Cassidy pressed.

"We were just hunting for frogs," Maddie supplied, trying to help. She felt horrible for putting Nick in this position. "And turtles sometimes."

"I didn't like the turtles," Nick said. "They bit. I only caught them because you were infatuated with them."

"I liked their painted shells," Maddie explained.

"So, you caught them for her?" Cassidy asked. "That's so nice. Was she scared to catch them herself?"

Nick took a sip from his water glass. "Maddie wasn't scared of catching them," he said. "She wasn't scared of animals. She baited her own hooks, and she caught her own fish. She even cleaned them herself."

"Oh, then why did you catch them for her?" Cassidy asked. She wasn't letting this go.

Nick was at a loss.

"They were too quick for me," Maddie said.

"Oh," Cassidy said, nodding. "That's really sweet."

Nick rubbed his hand over his forehead and brushed his dark hair out of his face. "We should probably order."

"You need a haircut," Christy said. "You should come in and let me trim it up."

"It's fine," Nick said. "I think you've done more than enough."

Christy snorted. "I haven't done anything but tell the truth."

Nick didn't have a chance to respond because the restaurant's owner, Ruby, arrived at the corner of the table just then with a weary expression and a notebook. She looked exactly the same. It was like stepping back in time. "Everyone ready to order?"

"Yes," Nick said. "I'll have a cheeseburger with mustard, pickles and onions. Put extra pickles on the side, please."

"You really shouldn't eat so much red meat," Cassidy chastised him.

"I'll consider it," Nick replied, refusing to look up from the paper placemat in front of him.

"I'll have a side salad with lemon juice," Cassidy said. "No cheese or croutons. Oh, and no bacon bits."

Ruby rolled her eyes and shifted her gaze to Christy. "Do you want your usual?"

"A burrito sounds good," Christy said. "Don't skimp on the sour cream."

"That's a lot of processed food," Cassidy said.

Christy ignored her.

Ruby lifted here eyes to Maddie, doing a double take when she realized who she was staring at. "Well, well, well," she said. "If it isn't Maddie Graves."

"Hi, Ruby," Maddie said, the smile on her face genuine for the first time that afternoon. "It's really good to see you."

"Well, girl, you grew up just how I pictured you would," Ruby said, studying her for a moment.

Maddie didn't know how to take that.

"In fact, you both grew up just how I pictured you," Ruby said, tapping her pen against the side of Nick's head. "You're like those people who pose for advertising photos." Ruby clucked appreciatively. "It's good to see you two together again. I never did get used to seeing Nick here without you attached to his hip."

Maddie opened her mouth to protest, but Ruby didn't give her a chance.

"So, do you want your regular? If I remember right, you always got a cheeseburger with ketchup and pickles – and then Nick here would always give you his extra pickles because they were your favorite."

"That sounds great," Maddie said, mostly because she was at a loss for anything else to say.

Once Ruby was gone, a pall settled over the table. Cassidy was the one who finally broke it. "So, I'm confused," she said. "Did you two date or not?"

"I told you we didn't," Nick said, scowling. "We were just friends."

"Except everyone in town seems to think you were more than that," Cassidy said. "There has to be a reason."

"I thought for sure you two would get married," Christy said, her gaze bouncing between Nick and Maddie curiously. "It was like you were soul mates."

"Soul mates?" Nick arched an eyebrow. "Do you believe in things like that?"

"I do," Christy said, her voice softening. "I still do."

"I do, too," Cassidy said, smiling brightly. She patted Nick's hand. "It's a really romantic thought."

Maddie's gaze lingered on Cassidy's hand as she rubbed her fingers on top of his knuckles. Nick's eyes followed, and he uncomfortably withdrew his hand and placed it on his lap.

"I think soul mates are a figment of people's imagination," he said.

"That's cynical," Cassidy said, hurt fitting through her heavy-lidded eyes. Maddie realized the woman thought Nick was her soul mate, so his pointed comments about soul mates were crushing her. She had no way of knowing that Nick was saying the words to hurt Maddie.

"It's the truth," Nick said, his dark eyes boring holes into Maddie's heart. "People aren't destined for each other. People find each other by luck, and then they build a relationship. It's work. It's not something you just luck into."

"But … ." Cassidy wasn't convinced.

Maddie pressed her lips together. "I agree with Nick," she said. "No matter how much you try to convince yourself that there's only one person for you, that's not reality."

"Oh, good grief," Christy muttered. "It's like being in high school drama class all over again."

Maddie shook her head, Christy's words sinking in. "You know what? I'm sorry. I forgot I have a previous engagement." She got to her feet and dug into her purse for some money. "Give my apologies to Ruby, and tell her I'll stop in when I have more time."

"Where are you going?" Cassidy asked.

"I have to … Granny needs me at home," Maddie said, making up a lie on the spot. "She's been having a hard time since my mother … died." Maddie's voice was raspy as she choked on the last word. "We … um … both have."

"You should eat something," Cassidy said. "You're far too thin. You probably haven't had a decent meal since your mother died. If you keep running yourself down, you'll never find the strength to pick yourself back up. I saw that on *Dr. Phil.*"

"Well, then you know it's good advice," Maddie said.

"I'll stop by and see you," Christy said. "I'll give you a little time to … get over this."

"There's nothing to get over," Maddie said hurriedly. "I … I'm fine."

"Maddie," Nick got to his feet to stop her, but Maddie was already striding toward the front door of the diner. "Maddie!"

Maddie felt as if she was being smothered. Even stepping outside the diner and gulping in huge mouthfuls of fresh air didn't relieve the pressure in her chest. She was drowning. That's what it felt like.

She was so lightheaded, Maddie had to lean against the brick diner exterior to keep her balance. The sound of the bell above the door jangling behind her caused her to jump. She risked a glance over her shoulder, half expecting to find Nick standing there with an angry expression on his face. When the spot was empty, signifying someone had entered the establishment, Maddie pushed herself around the corner of the building and into the alleyway that separated Ruby's Diner from Walker Hardware.

Maddie pressed her eyes shut and tried to regain her equilibrium. Coming home was so much worse than she thought it would be. No, that's not true. Coming home had been a mixed bag. Olivia was here, and Maude needed her, and seeing Christy had even been a nice surprise. What had her reeling was Nick.

She knew it would be difficult to see him. She just hadn't expected so much anger, or resentment, or ... Cassidy. Who names their daughter Cassidy anyway? Did her parents know she would grow up to look like a peaches-and-cream angel? Did God design her into a perfect little package just to torture her?

Maddie was having a hard time disliking Cassidy, even though everything about the woman bugged her. She was just too ... nice. If she was a bitch, like Marla, things would be so much easier. Hating Cassidy was a waste of energy. It was like hating a puppy. Who hates a puppy?

Still, Maddie wouldn't mind locking her up in a kennel and conveniently losing the key. Oh, that was an awful thing to think. *I don't have any claim on Nick.* Maddie kept telling herself that, even though her heart didn't seem to believe it.

When Maddie finally managed to wrench her eyes open and look around, she realized she wasn't alone in the alley. Unfortunately, the young woman standing a few feet away from her happened to be dead.

"Oh, no," Maddie muttered. It was happening again.

The woman didn't speak. Everything about her was immovable, from her strawberry blonde hair down to the bottom hem of her flowery dress.

Maddie took a step forward. "Are you lost? Do you need help?" She kept her voice low, not wanting to risk a passerby hearing. "Do you know your name?"

The woman didn't speak. Instead, she finally lifted her arm and pointed. Maddie followed the arch of her finger with her eyes, curious. When she registered what the woman was pointing at, the bottom fell out of her world. Again.

It really *was* happening again. The female entity was pointing at her own body, which was spread eagle on the ground and covered with blood. Maddie opened her mouth to yell, but no sound would come out.

"That's me," the woman said. "I'm Sarah Alden, and that's me. I can see me. Does this mean I'm dead? If I'm dead, why can you see me?"

Suddenly, Maddie's world was spinning, and her mind was screaming for ... *Nick!*

6. SIX

"Do you think she's okay?"

Cassidy's eyes were trained on the door Maddie had just fled through, concern etched on her face.

"I'm sure she's just ... shaken up," Christy said.

"Why would she be shaken up?" Cassidy asked. "Is it because she's still mourning her mother? That must be it. Other than her grandmother, Olivia was the only family she had, right?"

"Yeah," Christy said. "It was just the three of them."

Nick was lost in thought. He was still standing. It was like he was waiting for Maddie to come back. Waiting wasn't the right word. No, he was hoping she would come back. He was hoping she would come back and let him apologize. He was hoping ... .

"What happened to her father?" Cassidy asked.

Nick jerked back to reality. "He abandoned Olivia and his daughter when Maddie was just a baby."

"That's horrible."

"It is horrible," Nick said, clenching his jaw. He reached into his wallet and dropped a few bills on the table. "I need to get going."

"What about lunch?" Cassidy looked crushed.

"I ... I have some things I have to get done," Nick said. "I forgot about them. I'm sorry."

"It's okay," Cassidy said. "I was surprised to see you in the first place." She lifted her face up and smiled at him. "Give me a kiss before you go."

Nick's stomach twisted. It wasn't her fault, but the idea of kissing Cassidy – especially in front of Christy – unsettled him. Instead of pressing his lips to hers, he dropped a hesitant kiss on top of her head and patted her shoulder. "I'll ... call you later."

Nick didn't miss the disappointed look on Cassidy's face.

"Okay," she said.

Nick strode toward the door, internally cursing himself for hurting Cassidy. She was a sweet girl. She'd never done a thing to warrant being mistreated, and yet the idea of touching her now was ... uncomfortable. It hadn't been a problem until Maddie had reentered his life twenty-four hours before. Until then, things had been fine. His relationship with Cassidy wasn't the stuff of great romance books – or even maudlin movies – but it had been comfortable.

Now nothing felt comfortable in his life.

When Nick hit Main Street in front of Ruby's Diner, he found himself scanning the bustling storefronts. He told himself he wasn't looking for Maddie, but he knew it wasn't true. He just wanted to make sure she was okay. Her face had been so ... broken ... when she fled. He was partially to blame, but he was just so angry with her. He knew it was irrational. Who holds a grudge for something a teenager did ten years later? *The one who was left behind, that's who.*

Nick sighed. Maddie was gone. She'd been gone, he reminded himself. Just because she was physically back, that didn't mean she was emotionally back. It didn't mean she'd come home for him. It didn't mean ... . Nick paused when a hint of movement caught his attention out of the corner of his eye.

He shifted his shoulders, sucking in a breath when he saw Maddie. She was standing halfway down the alley, her gaze focused on the ground a few feet in front of her. There was something ... odd ... about the situation. Instinctively, Nick moved toward her.

"Maddie?"

She didn't answer him.

"Maddie, I'm sorry for ... the weird lunch." Had he pushed her so far she was hiding in an alley? That was so wrong.

When Maddie didn't respond again, Nick studied her more closely. Her face was ashen, and her chest was heaving with shallow movements, as if each breath she took was painful. Something was wrong.

Nick rushed forward and grabbed her arm, snapping her body around so she was facing him. "Maddie!"

Maddie's blue eyes were scattered. "N-nick."

"What's wrong?"

Maddie threw her arms around his neck, and Nick didn't fight the embrace. He tightened his arms around her, hating the way her body shook as melded to him. "Mad, what's wrong?"

Maddie didn't move her head from Nick's chest, instead extending her arm and pointing to a spot on the ground a few feet away. Nick moved Maddie's hair out of the way so he could see what she was pointing at and then sucked in a breath. "Oh, shit."

THE BLACKSTONE Bay Police Department arrived en masse within five minutes. Since the department consisted of three police officers and one part-time police chief – who also served as the town mailman – Maddie wasn't surprised by the quick response.

Nick had kept Maddie close, even when he checked to make sure the woman was dead. It was fairly obvious emergency personnel wouldn't be needed. The wounds on her torso were deep, and the blood pooled on her chest had dried sometime during the night. She was beyond help – at least of the physical kind.

Once his co-workers arrived, Nick shuffled Maddie to the sidewalk. She was in shock, but she still needed to be questioned. After taping off the crime scene, and calling the coroner, Nick rejoined Maddie as another officer, Dale Kreskin, questioned her.

"What made you go down the alley?"

Maddie worried her bottom lip with her teeth. "I was ... just looking for a moment to collect myself."

"Why?"

Maddie looked to Nick for help, unsure how to answer. "I was just a little ... unhinged after lunch."

"And why is that?" Dale asked.

"I ... um ... it's just been hard to reintegrate myself back into town," Maddie said, squaring her shoulders. "I keep running into people I used to know."

"And who were you having lunch with?"

"Christy Ford."

"Just her?"

"And ... um ... Cassidy ... ." Maddie shot a furtive look in Nick's direction. "I don't know her last name."

"Dunham," Nick supplied.

"*Your* Cassidy?" Dale asked.

Nick didn't miss the face Maddie made. It was a quick reaction, and she pushed it away as fast as she could, but he'd still seen it. It made him feel ... something. "Yes," he said. "I was there, too."

"Do you two know each other?" Dale hadn't grown up in the area, only coming to Blackstone Bay after twenty years with the Detroit Police Department, so he wasn't familiar with a lot of the local history. While Dale had been bored with the lack of crime in town during his five-year tenure, Nick was happy someone with so much experience was here now.

"We grew up together," Nick said evasively. "We were just getting ... reacquainted."

Dale's keen brown eyes bounced between Maddie and Nick, curious. "Uh-huh."

"Is that all you need?" Maddie asked.

"I guess so," Dale said. "I need a number to reach you at in case I have more questions. You're not planning on leaving town, are you?"

"No," Maddie said. She gave him her cell phone number. When he was gone, she let loose with a shaky sigh and blessed Nick with a watery smile. "Well, this was quite the welcome home."

Nick reached out and pushed her hair away from her face. It was still as soft as he remembered, as was the skin his fingers brushed against with the movement. "Are you okay, Mad?"

Maddie stilled. "I ... don't know. It's just all so surreal."

Nick nodded sympathetically. He pulled her in close, his body overriding the warnings his mind kept screaming and gave her another hug. Something told him she needed the solace – and he just couldn't stop himself. He wanted to touch her.

Maddie burrowed her face into the hollow between his neck and chest. Nick pressed his cheek to the top of her head, and then he proceeded to rock back and forth to lull her – just like he had when Marla Proctor terrorized Maddie back in high school. It was as if nothing had changed. Even the steady beat of her heart was the same.

"It's going to be okay, Mad."

CASSIDY COULDN'T STOP the feeling of dread from dwarfing her as she watched Nick console Maddie from the front stoop of Ruby's Diner. He hadn't even bothered to look for her in the melee surrounding the discovery. It was like she didn't exist.

Cassidy had seen him, though. He'd only left Maddie's side when forced, returning as quickly as he could and ... touching her every chance he got. Cassidy didn't miss that. Nick's hands seemed to have a mind of their own, and that mind was focused on Maddie.

Before Maddie returned to town, Cassidy had pushed her misgivings about the woman as far down into her soul as she could manage. She'd heard the whispers. *Stay away from Nick Winters. He'll never want anyone but Maddie Graves.* Since Cassidy had no idea who Maddie was, she'd ignored the rumors because she was desperate to get close to Nick.

Who wouldn't want to be close to him? He was all muscles and bright smiles. He had the face of a Greek god, and the body of a movie star. He was sweet, and nice, and even romantic from time to time. Sure, his mind often seemed to wander, but it always returned to her eventually.

Cassidy had a feeling something was different now. Nick had lied to her. She was sure of that. He claimed he didn't want her to go down to Willow Lake with him because it was his "thinking" place. He said he always went down there alone. Now she knew why he really disappeared there three times a week: That was where he felt closest to Maddie.

Cassidy's heart was beating so hard she was sure it was about to explode. Nick said they'd never dated – and she believed him – but she knew now it wasn't because he didn't want to date the willowy blonde. She also knew it wasn't because Maddie didn't want Nick. They were both obviously too scared to admit their feelings.

Her world was slipping away, and she was just standing there watching it happen. Nick's face was buried in Maddie's hair, and his hands were tight around her back as he rocked her in his arms. Cassidy knew Nick had never held her that way, or looked at her the way he did when Maddie fled from lunch. He'd never felt anything for her like he did for Maddie.

"I'm sure it's not what you think," Christy said, appearing at Cassidy's elbow.

Cassidy collected herself. "And what am I thinking?"

"You're thinking that they're ... having an affair or something," Christy said. "Nick isn't the kind of guy who cheats."

Cassidy pursed her lips. "Are you telling me they don't have feelings for each other?"

Christy tilted her head to the side. "No."

"Well, thanks for being honest," Cassidy said.

"I'm sorry," Christy said. "I try not to lie. You should just prepare yourself."

"For what? Do you think Nick is going to leave me in the dust now that Maddie is back in town? Do you think they're going to pick up where they left off?" Cassidy was desperate for Christy to tell her she was overreacting.

"You're a nice woman, Cassidy," Christy said. "You were never really in the game where Nick was concerned, though."

"What are you talking about? We've been dating for six months." Cassidy was crushed.

"But he's been in love with Maddie since he was seventeen," Christy said.

"They haven't seen each other in ten years," Cassidy argued.

"That doesn't mean they haven't loved each other all of that time," Christy said. "Listen, I don't want to hurt you. Nick doesn't want to hurt you either. He's not that kind of guy. That doesn't change the fact that he's always been in love with Maddie. You need to … ."

"Prepare myself," Cassidy said, bitter. "You already told me that."

"It will be easier to let him go now."

"I don't want to let him go," Cassidy said. "I'm in love with him."

"But he's in love with her."

"He hasn't said anything like that to me," Cassidy pointed out. "You can't possibly know that he's in love with her."

"Has he told you that he loves you?" Christy asked, changing tactics.

"No," Cassidy hedged.

"Have you told him that you love him?"

Cassidy nodded, her lower lip trembling.

"And how does he respond when you say it?" Christy asked.

"He … changes the subject." Christy pressed her lips together, and Cassidy could read the sympathy on the woman's round face. She hated it. She hated the pity. "I'm not giving up on him," she said, resolute.

"Okay," Christy said. "That's your decision."

Cassidy turned her attention back to the street, her heart sinking when she saw Nick wrap his arm around Maddie's shoulders so he could lead her in the opposite direction from the crime scene. She watched them go – they seemed lost in their own little world, their heads bent together as they talked – and her heart broke.

She knew, deep down, that Christy was right. That didn't mean she was going to let Nick just walk away and run into the arms of the town's resident bombshell. No, what she had to do was step up her game. Cassidy was determined to claim Nick as her own, and she wasn't going to let Maddie stand in her way. Nothing was going to stand in her way.

7. SEVEN

"Thanks for giving me a ride home," Maddie said, shifting in the passenger seat of Nick's truck and fixing him with a small smile as they idled. "You didn't have to. I would've walked. It was only a few blocks."

"You were a little shaken up," Nick said. "I don't blame you. It's not every day that you stumble across a dead body – especially in Blackstone Bay."

"No," Maddie agreed, rubbing her temple to ward off an imminent headache. "You expect it in the city. You don't expect it here."

Nick smirked. "Did you see a lot of dead bodies when you were down south?"

"Just a few," Maddie murmured.

Nick stilled. "Are you being serious? I can't tell."

Maddie shook her head. "Oh, sorry, I was just … ."

"Maddie, tell me what you were just thinking," Nick prodded.

Maddie searched his face, fighting the urge to reach out and touch it. When they were younger, she couldn't stop herself from touching him. Even now, that's all she really wanted to do. "I was just thinking that my life is … a mess."

"Why?"

"Because I made it that way," Maddie replied, shrugging.

"How?"

Maddie averted her eyes from his. It made it easier to fight the urge to touch him. "You know, when I left Blackstone Bay, I had no intention of coming back. I thought … I thought it would be so much easier to start a new life in a place where no one knew me. I just didn't want to be … me."

"What was so bad about being you, Mad? I happened to like you a great deal."

"You were the only one."

"That's not true," Nick said.

"It is," Maddie said. "All I had was you, and Mom, and Granny … and a world of people who looked down on me."

Nick rolled his neck, cracking it as he bobbed his head. "Maddie, I'm not saying that growing up here was easy for you, but it wasn't as hard as you seem to remember. I know there were some girls – stupid Marla Proctor – who terrorized you. They didn't hate you because they looked down on you, though. They hated you because they were jealous of you. You just don't seem to realize it. That's high school, though. You're an adult now."

"I don't feel like an adult," Maddie said, pushing the rest of his statement out of her mind so she could mull it over later.

"What made you decide to come home?" Nick asked. "Was it really just because Olivia died?"

"No," Maddie said. "I've spent the past five years wanting to come home."

"You have?" Nick seemed surprised. "Why didn't you just come home then?"

"I was scared to," Maddie admitted.

"What's so scary, Mad?"

Maddie didn't answer him, at least not head on. "When I left, I didn't think I was running away from anything. I really didn't. I thought I was running toward something."

"What were you running toward?"

"Freedom."

"And did you find that?"

"Not in the least," Maddie said. "I found … nothing. It wasn't what I thought it would be. Once I was out in the real world, I just wanted to … come home."

"Why didn't you?"

"I was scared to see you," Maddie said, her voice small.

Nick shifted in his seat. "Why? Was it because of the way you left?"

"I need you to know, I never meant to hurt you," Maddie said, lifting her tear-filled eyes so they were even with his. "I just thought it would be easier. I used to sit by the phone and wait for you to call when I was in college. It was … painful. Then we'd talk for twenty minutes, and I would be miserable the whole week waiting for you to call again."

"I wasn't happy either," Nick said. "I missed you. I missed you a heck of a lot more when you stopped taking my phone calls."

"I thought a clean break would be easier for both of us," Maddie said. "I knew you would have no problem moving on."

"Then you didn't know me at all," Nick said, his body stiffening.

Maddie took that as her cue to leave. "I really am sorry, Nicky. I wouldn't hurt you for anything. You're one of the only three people in my life I've ever … loved. I'm sorry."

Maddie climbed out of the truck and slammed the door quickly, cutting off any response Nick might have. She didn't want to hear it. She couldn't hear it. She was just … overwhelmed.

Maddie raced toward the house, her mind registering the sound of Nick's truck as it backed out of the driveway, but her heart was racing so fast she felt like she was about to pass out. It took every ounce of energy she had not to turn around and beg him to stay. He wasn't hers, not anymore. Well, truth be told, he'd never really been hers.

That didn't stop her from missing him – or desperately dreaming of a life where they were together.

It just wasn't in the cards. She had to move on.

. . .

NICK WANTED TO CHASE HER. He wanted to grab her. He wanted to shake her. He wanted to ... kiss her until her lips were raw. *Dammit!*

Nick didn't do any of those things. Instead, he slammed his truck into reverse and sped out of her driveway. He didn't make it far. He pulled his truck to the side of the road about a hundred feet away – in a spot where he knew the trees would hide his vehicle should Maddie look out the windows – and then he lowered his forehead to the steering wheel.

He couldn't take this. It was too much. Seeing her again ... having her so close that he could touch her ... it was driving him insane. He was still angry. No, he was furious. It was hard to stay mad, though. Her face, it broke him every time. It was like watching an angel fall. She was so sad, so miserable, so ... lost. He wanted to help her find herself, but it wasn't his job.

Knowing that, feeling it to his very core, he couldn't understand why he wasn't leaving. Nick had no idea. He just knew he couldn't drive away. Not yet. Something was keeping him here, and it wasn't just Maddie's magnetic pull. It was something else.

So, he rested his head against the seat in his truck ... and he waited.

MADDIE COULDN'T FACE Maude while she was so unsettled. Instead, she sank down onto the front steps of the house and rested her head against the wrought-iron banister.

She hadn't been lying – or exaggerating – when she told Nick her life was a mess. Her life had been nothing but a mess since leaving Blackstone Bay. First up was college, where she'd been miserable for the entire run of her nursing degree. She'd kept her nose to the grindstone, held a menial job at the bookstore on the side, and graduated without making a single friend who stuck.

Once she graduated, she got a job in suburban Detroit and moved to the southeastern part of the state, where she proceeded to work sixty hours a week – every week – and pretend that it didn't bother her that she didn't have a life.

For a time, a very short time, she put herself out into the dating world. Doctors were always asking her out. The nursing pool was easy for them to delve into, so she accepted a few dates, even managing to engage in a sexual relationship with a handful of them. She was still miserable, though, and she ceased her dating life as fast as she started it. She just wasn't interested.

Then something happened. A woman with catastrophic injuries came into the emergency room. She was declared brain dead, and her family refused to pull the plug, even though the woman's spirit was trapped while they agonized over the decision. Maddie saw her every day for a week, and she ignored her every day for that week. The woman was tortured, desperate for her family to let her go, and yet her family refused to believe she was gone.

Finally, on the last day of the woman's life, Maddie couldn't take it anymore. The police were at the hospital to give the family an update, one that didn't include happy news of an arrest, and Maddie inadvertently blurted out the fact that the individual who had run her off the road was actually her estranged husband.

Maddie regretted the words the second they came out of her mouth, and Officer Dean Kincaid was utterly suspicious of her for the rest of the afternoon. When he overheard Maddie tell the family how desperate the woman was to pass on, he cornered her to ask about her abilities.

Maddie initially feigned ignorance. Her mother had instilled the need for secrecy into her at a very young age. That's why she'd never told Nick what she could do. What would he have said if she told him? How would that conversation even go? Maddie knew, without a doubt, no matter how loyal Nick was, he would never be able to understand that not only could she see and talk to ghosts – but she also had a sixth sense that allowed her to find certain things, including missing people. He would've thought she was lying – and crazy – and she couldn't bear to see the disappointment on his face. She preferred to remember the way he used to look at her, like she was fun and eccentric – and his very best friend in the world. Those were the memories she clung to.

After the woman died at the hospital, Kincaid started showing up with case files. He wasn't sure exactly how Maddie's "peculiarity" worked, but he was convinced he could use it to his advantage. Maddie ignored him for a long time, but when he came to her with a missing person's case involving a small child, Maddie couldn't turn away.

She found the eight-year-old girl chained to a radiator in the basement of an abandoned building in Detroit in less than five hours. She helped find the suspect involved in the kidnapping two hours later. After that, Kincaid was on her doorstep once a week – no matter how hard Maddie protested. That lasted for two years, until ... well ... it suddenly stopped.

Maddie shook her head. She didn't want to think about that. Not now. Not ever again.

Maddie lifted her head, her resolve strengthened enough to consider going into the house. Magicks was still a mess, and if she planned on reopening on time next week, she was going to have to get moving on the inventory and cleaning. Now was as good of a time as any.

Olivia was watching Maddie, clear blue eyes studying her, when she got to her feet.

"Mom. What's going on?"

"I was just wondering that myself," Olivia said. "Why are you sitting out here?"

"I was just .... "

"Collecting yourself, I know," Olivia said. "You did it all the time when you were a kid – and especially when you were a teenager. You never wanted me to know when you were upset, so you'd sit out here for hours until you convinced yourself that I wouldn't notice how red and puffy your eyes were."

"You knew that?" Maddie was stunned.

"Of course I knew that. I'm your mother."

"Why didn't you tell me?"

Olivia shrugged. "You didn't want me to know. I figured you'd come to me eventually, but you never did. Do you want to tell me what's wrong today?"

Maddie recounted her afternoon, not leaving a thing out. When she was done, Olivia was smiling. It wasn't the reaction she was expecting. "A woman is dead. I don't think it's very funny."

"Of course it's not funny," Olivia replied. "That's not why I was smiling."

"Why were you smiling?"

"I just like to see you and Nick working your way back to each other."

"We're not working our way back to each other," Maddie said, annoyed. "He's got a girlfriend. Did you miss that part of the conversation?"

"No," Olivia said. "I'm sure she's a lovely girl. I hope she's not hurt too much when Nick dumps her."

"Why is Nick going to dump her?"

"Oh, sunshine, that was set in stone the minute you stepped back into this town," Olivia said. "Nick won't be able to stay away from you. He never could."

"Nick hates me, Mom."

"He's hurt and angry," Olivia countered. "He doesn't hate you. He could never hate you."

"Are you suddenly omnipotent now that you're dead?" Maddie challenged.

"That's not ghost powers, sunshine," Olivia said. "That's mom powers. Come on. Let's take a walk. You'll feel better once you burn off some of this excess energy."

"I don't want to take a walk."

"Well, you're going to," Olivia said. "I'm still your mother. Now, get your butt in gear, young lady. I don't want to sit here and watch you mope for one more second."

"You know, once you're dead, you can't boss me around anymore," Maddie said. "That's a rule."

Olivia ignored her. "March!"

. . .

NICK LIFTED his head when he saw Maddie trudge into the woods that surrounded the backside of her family's property. She appeared to be talking to someone – but she was alone.

That was ... odd.

It's none of your business, Nick told himself. If she wants to wander around the woods talking to herself, you don't care. She's probably going crazy. The guilt from leaving him had driven her over the edge. That should make him happy. She deserved it.

Nick was out of his truck before he realized what he was doing, and he was halfway into the woods before he acknowledged that he was following her. He just had to know who she was talking to.

After a few minutes of treading lightly – he didn't want her to hear him, after all – he heard Maddie's melodious voice.

"I am not pouting."

Who is she talking to? Nick cocked his head to the side so he could listen harder. No one was answering her, though.

"I don't care what you say," Maddie said. "You're being idiotic." Silence. "I'm not calling you an idiot. I'm saying you're being idiotic." More silence. "Oh, I can, too. You're just trying to aggravate me."

Nick moved out of the trees and stepped into the small meadow where Maddie was busily picking wildflowers. She continued to chatter away, but a steady scan told Nick she was alone. He started to feel uncomfortable, so he cleared his throat to alert Maddie to his presence.

He watched her body stiffen, and when she swiveled, her face was awash with embarrassment.

"What are you doing here?" Maddie asked.

"I saw you go into the woods."

"And you followed me?"

"It looked like ... were you just talking to someone?"

Maddie's face was a mask of horror and doubt. "I was ... talking to myself."

"And what were you saying?"

"Well ... what did you hear me say?"

"You were calling someone an idiot."

"Oh, I did not call her an idiot," Maddie snapped. "I said ... wait ... were you watching my house?"

Nick faltered. "I was sitting in my truck down the road."

"Why?"

"I was just thinking," Nick said, angry at being put on the defensive. She was the one acting like a freak. "Who were you talking to?"

Maddie scowled. "If you must know, I was talking to my mother."

Nick blew out a sigh, relieved. "Oh, you were pretending to have a conversation with your mom because of everything that happened today," he said, filling in the gaps so Maddie wouldn't have to.

"Yeah, that's it," Maddie said, her tone droll. "I just ... it makes me feel closer to her."

"I understand that, Mad," Nick said. "I just ... I was worried about you."

"Well, you don't have to be," Maddie said. "I'm not crazy."

"I didn't say you were crazy."

"Well ... I'm not."

"Okay."

"Great."

"Good."

Nick had nothing left to say after that, and Maddie wasn't volunteering any further information, so he left. He was sure the loss of Olivia had thrown Maddie for a loop. It made sense that she needed someone to talk to. A lot of people talked to dead relatives, didn't they? Of course, most people probably didn't hold entire conversations, like someone else was speaking back to them, but Maddie had gone through a trauma that afternoon. It was to be expected.

So how come Nick didn't really believe that?

8. EIGHT

The thing Maddie loved most about Blackstone Bay was the kitschy atmosphere. The town didn't change, the storefronts were still the same as they were ten years before (and twenty years before that, truth be told), and the town didn't show signs of growing pains. It was small enough to be claustrophobic, but the boundaries of the country fields and woods that surrounded it were wide enough to let fresh air in.

Maddie was home, and she hadn't been this ... relaxed ... in a very long time. She was sure happiness would follow. Somehow.

After spending four hours toiling in Magicks, even getting on all fours to scrub the corners of the floor with a bucket and brush, Maddie needed a break. She decided to treat herself to an ice cream cone from Fletcher's Soda Shoppe, take a walk through town, and then return for a couple more hours of work.

The body discovery from the previous afternoon was still the topic of conversation on everyone's lips, although the victim's identity wasn't public yet, and after answering a few uncomfortable questions at Fletcher's, Maddie escaped to the street with her ice cream. While the woman's death plagued her, Nick's appearance in the meadow was what was really bothering her. *How much had he heard? Had he really believed she was out there talking to herself?*

Maddie pinched the bridge of her nose. This was exactly what she'd been afraid of. This was exactly why she'd pushed him away. If he found out, he would never look at her in the same way. She wouldn't be Maddie, the girl he spent his childhood playing with. She would be Maddie, the freak who thought she could talk to ghosts. It was mortifying.

Summer hadn't technically hit Blackstone Bay. It was still weeks away, but late spring in Michigan is a beautiful time, and Maddie relished the feeling of the sun on her skin as she wandered around the small downtown area. After finishing her treat, she discarded her refuse in a garbage can. She straightened when a shadow moved over her, lifting her head to ready herself for another barrage of questions about the body.

The man standing in front of her was familiar – and yet different. His brown hair was shorter than she remembered, but his jaw was still square and set. The planes of his cheekbones were still high and pronounced. His body was still tall and trim. All those things were the same. *So, what was different?* Instead of a football jersey, he was dressed in an expensive suit and leather loafers. His eyes were an amazing powder blue, but there was no mischief flirting in their depths. He looked more ... mature.

Todd Winthrop. He'd graduated from Blackstone Bay High School the same year Maddie and Nick had matriculated. He was the town's prodigal son. He was the star running back on the football team, earning a scholarship to Michigan State University for his field prowess. He'd graduated with top honors, been the president of her senior class, and he was every teenage girl's dream – well, other than Nick.

Maddie hadn't crossed paths with Todd often. He and Nick were competitive, and Maddie's loyalty had always been with Nick. As teenagers, Todd went out of his way to flirt with her, but Maddie knew it was because he was trying to get a dig in at Nick, not because he was genuinely interested in her.

"Hello, Todd," Maddie said, smiling shyly.

"Maddie Graves," Todd said, smiling down at her. "I heard rumors you were back in town. I didn't believe them until I saw it with my own eyes, though."

"The rumors are true."

"You look ... amazing." Todd's eyes were bright with intrigue as he looked her up and down, taking in her cutoff shorts and T-shirt with studied interest. "You haven't changed a bit."

"Well, I hope that's not true," Maddie said, shifting uncomfortably. "I would hate to think I was stuck in time."

"Being stuck in time isn't a bad thing, Miss Maddie," he said, his tone teasing. "Especially when you look *that*."

"Like what?"

"Like you stepped right off of a runway," Todd said.

"Oh, you're quite the flatterer."

"You're worth the flattery."

The duo made small talk for a few minutes, Todd telling Maddie about the car dealership he'd opened on the outskirts of town three years before, and Maddie carefully stepping around the end of her nursing career. The conversation was light and comfortable.

"So, I can't say I'm not surprised to find you still living in Blackstone Bay," Maddie said. "I thought for sure you would hit a big city by storm and never look back."

Todd pursed his lips together and shrugged. "Blackstone Bay is home. It's a great town."

"It is," Maddie agreed. "That's why I came back."

Todd narrowed his eyes thoughtfully. "Is that the only reason you came back?"

"I'm not sure what you mean," Maddie hedged.

Todd shifted his gaze to the police station across the road. The single-story building, red brick walls and black roof, was bright beneath the afternoon sun. Maddie hadn't even realized where she was. Well ... mostly.

"I still don't know what you mean."

"So, all of those rumors about you and Nick Winters in high school were wrong?" Todd asked.

"I'm not sure what rumors you're referring to," Maddie said. "We were friends. What else was being gossiped about?" Maddie had already gotten an earful from Christy, but she was mildly curious if Todd would be forthcoming or coy.

"The ones where you and Winters were out fornicating in the woods every night of our high school career."

Well, so much for him being coy. "Like I said, we were just friends."

"And what about now?" Todd asked.

"Now we're ... acquaintances."

"Oh, so all the people on the streets saying that Winters was glued to your side after you discovered a dead body in the alley between the hardware store and the diner were exaggerating?"

It was a pointed question. "He was doing his job."

Todd held his hands up in mock surrender. "Okay. I was just asking. I didn't want to step on anyone's toes."

Maddie wrinkled her nose. "What toes?"

The smile that moved across Todd's face was a mixture of play and prey. "Well, since I'm going to ask you out to dinner, I want to make sure I'm not poaching on anyone's ... property."

Maddie's mouth dropped open. "I ... um ... ."

"I'm going to take that as a yes," Todd said, not giving her a chance to come up with an excuse to bow out. He reached over and brushed a strand of Maddie's flyaway hair away from her face. "You're kind of cute when you're nervous."

Maddie squared her shoulders. "What makes you think I'm nervous?"

Todd grinned, letting his dimple come out to play. "Oh, you're not? Good. I'll pick you up at seven."

"I CAN'T DO THIS," Maddie said, her voice rising an octave. "I don't want to do this."

"You can do it, girl," Maude said, holding a floral dress up next to

Maddie's face and then shaking her head in disgust. "Why does everything in your closet look like the Amish should be wearing it?"

"There's nothing wrong with that dress," Maddie complained.

"Maddie, you're twenty-eight years old," Maude said. "You shouldn't dress like you're fifty. Don't you have anything that shows off your body?"

"No."

"Everyone calm down," Christy said, breezing into Maddie's upstairs bedroom with a pile of clothes over her arm and a makeup case in her hand. "I'm here. Everything is going to be fine."

Maddie wrinkled her nose. "How did you get in?"

"Everyone knows you keep the key in that ceramic turtle on the front porch," Christy said, looking Maddie up and down. "You can't wear that."

Maddie self-consciously crossed her arms over her chest to hide her bra. "I know."

"That's what you show him at the end of the date," Christy said. She tossed her makeup kit on Maddie's bed and started rummaging through the clothes she'd brought. "I went through all the clothes I've bought over the years thinking that one day I would be thin enough to wear them. Something in here will work."

"Good," Maude said, crumpling the dress she was holding into a ball and dumping it in the garbage can by the vanity. "We have to take this girl shopping."

"My clothes are fine," Maddie protested. "They're comfortable."

"Honey, with legs like yours, you shouldn't be worried about being comfortable," Christy said. "You need to show them off." She grabbed a black dress out of the pile. "Put this on."

Maddie snorted. "That dress will never fit me."

"Put it on," Christy ordered.

Maddie scowled but did as she was told. The dress was light and airy. It boasted a flirty skirt that fell just above her knee, and it had spaghetti straps that held up a drooping neckline that displayed way too much cleavage. "Absolutely not."

"Do you have a strapless bra?" Christy asked, ignoring Maddie's protests. "You have an outstanding body, but your boobs are a lot smaller than mine. I don't have anything you can use."

Maude was already rummaging through Maddie's drawers. "Here."

Christy caught the small scrap of material Maude flung across the room. "Put this on."

"I can't wear this," Maddie said. "I look like a ... streetwalker."

"You look like a vision," Christy countered. "Put that on. I'll plug the curling iron in and we'll get going on your makeup."

"I don't really wear makeup."

"And that's why you don't need a lot of it," Christy said. "Trust me. Now, put that bra on. I don't want to hear another word out of you."

CHRISTY WATCHED MADDIE FIDGET. She'd always thought the stunning blonde was just being modest when it came to her looks. Sure, she'd been gawky in middle school, but everyone was. Once Maddie blossomed in high school, she'd turned into the prettiest girl in town – and never once acknowledged it.

After spending limited time with Maddie as an adult, Christy had come to the conclusion that Maddie was not being modest. She was just oblivious. Maddie honestly had no idea how beautiful she was. She had no idea how she affected men. It was kind of ... cute.

The black dress hit all of Maddie's curves in just the right way. Maddie was lithe, and she obviously worked out a great deal. She still had the kind of body that sent men on a path of sin without a backward glance.

After ten minutes of makeup lessons, and twenty minutes with the curling iron, Christy had finished by piling Maddie's hair on top of her head and securing it with an antique barrette from Maude's dresser. The loose curls Christy had layered throughout Maddie's hair were spilling out from a high pile on the back of her head. She looked ... breathtaking.

"You're going to knock him on his ass," Maude said. She leaned over and ran her fingers over Maddie's bare legs, nodding when she was done. "Good. You shaved your legs."

"What does that matter?"

"You can't sleep with a man if you don't shave your legs."

"I'm not going to sleep with him," Maddie said, scandalized. "I don't even *know* him."

"Of course you're not going to sleep with him," Maude said. "He might get handsy, though, and you need to be ready."

"Granny, please, don't make me do this," Maddie said, her blue eyes wide and pleading. "I don't even like him."

"Then why did you agree to go?" Christy asked.

"I didn't really agree to go," Maddie admitted. "He just kind of ... made me."

"Well, that's the only way to get you to do anything," Maude said. "You're too skittish to ever do anything on your own."

"I am not skittish."

"Girl, you're as skittish as a stray colt with wolves on its tail," Maude replied. She patted Maddie's arm. "You're going to be fine. If he gets fresh, just sock him in the mouth."

Maddie looked unsure, but all further protests died on her lips when the sound of a car horn caught everyone's attention.

"Your date is here," Maude said, grabbing Maddie's hand and dragging her down the stairs.

It took some effort, but Christy and Maude managed to push Maddie through the door – and then proceeded to watch her until they were sure she was safely in the passenger seat of Todd's Dodge Charger. Once the car disappeared from the driveway, Christy turned to Maude with a dubious look.

"You know Todd Winthrop is all hands and a snakelike tongue, right?"

"I've heard," Maude said, wrinkling her nose.

"Why did you push Maddie to go out with him? He's not her type."

"He's a jackass," Maude said. "Maddie still needs some socialization. Plus, a couple of dates with a lowlife like Todd will make her realize that Nick is worth fighting for."

"Oh, are you really worried those two won't find their way to each other?" Christy asked. "I had lunch with them yesterday, and let me tell you something, they're one hot-and-steamy run-in away from stripping naked and mounting each other in the middle of town."

"Hey, fresh mouth," Maude said, slapping Christy's hand. "I don't want them to just have sex. I want them to be ... happy."

"Trust me, Maude, they're not going to be able to stay away from each other," Christy said. "The only obstacle in their way is Cassidy. I feel a little bad for her."

"Why do you say that?"

"She was watching them yesterday," Christy said. "They didn't see her. In fact, Nick wasn't even aware she was on the same planet because he was too busy trying to take care of Maddie after she discovered that body."

Maude was intrigued. "Did she say something?"

"No," Christy said. "You could just tell by the look on her face. She knows she's already lost him."

"Then she should let him go," Maude said.

"She's not going to do that," Christy said. "She's still trying to convince herself that she has a shot."

"Well, it's just going to hurt more over the long haul," Maude said. "I've always known that Nick and Maddie were destined to be together. Now we just have to wait for the two of them to pull their heads out of their own behinds and give into their feelings."

"Oh, they'll get there," Christy said, smiling. "Once word gets out that Todd and Maddie went on a date, Nick is going to go nuclear."

"Well, that will be fun to watch," Maude said. "Do you want some lemonade?"

"Sure," Christy said. "I want to hang out here long enough to make sure Maddie doesn't just circle around and sneak back into the house."

"That is an unfortunate possibility," Maude agreed. "We really need to work on that girl's self-esteem."

"Don't worry," Christy said. "I think once Nick falls into place, other things are going to fall into place, too. She's still finding herself."

"I like how optimistic you are."

"I'm just a sucker for a happy ending," Christy said.

9. NINE

Maddie was so nervous she thought she was going to climb out of her own skin. The ride to the restaurant had been long – and uncomfortable. Todd had insisted on taking her down the coast to a cozy little seafood restaurant she'd never heard of before.

Maddie would've been more comfortable with a burger and some fries.

Thankfully for her, Todd managed to handle almost all of the conversation over the duration of their drive. Maddie occasionally nodded, or interjected a single word, but Todd was more than happy talking about himself for a half hour straight.

Maddie was already bored.

When they got to the restaurant, Todd insisted on racing around to open her door. "Did I tell you how amazing you look tonight?"

Maddie was still self-conscious about the dress. "I feel naked."

"That's why you look amazing." Todd snaked an arm around Maddie's waist and guided her through the front door. After charming the hostess, and slipping her a fifty because he hadn't made a reservation, the duo found themselves at a table by the window with drinks in their hands.

"This is a great place," Maddie said, licking her lips. "It must be new."

"It used to be an old boathouse," Todd said. "They renovated it about five years ago. The food is amazing. I highly recommend the lobster."

Maddie smiled. "Do you bring all of your dates here?"

"Are you asking if I date around a lot?"

"Maybe."

"I'm not a monk, if that's what you're asking," Todd said. "I don't think I date more than anyone else my age, though. I probably don't even date as much as you."

Maddie knew that wasn't true. "I don't really date."

"Oh, you're teasing me," Todd said, smiling. "No one who looks like you can go through life without dating."

Maddie sipped from her soda. "You'd be surprised."

"Is that why you're so nervous?" Todd asked, leaning back in his chair and scorching Maddie with a predatory look.

"I'm not nervous." She was beyond nervous.

"You might relax a little if you had something a little more ... adult ... to drink," Todd suggested. "How about a glass of wine?"

"Wine goes right to my head."

"Is that a bad thing?" Todd pressed. "I'm the one driving."

"I'm fine with my Diet Coke."

"Well, maybe with dinner," Todd said, glancing around the restaurant for a moment before returning his attention to Maddie. "So, tell me about yourself."

"What do you want to know?"

"Why did you leave nursing?"

Ah, there it was. "I just realized it wasn't for me."

"Shouldn't you have realized that when you were in college?"

"Probably," Maddie said. "I thought it was what I really wanted to do, but it turns out I couldn't take all of the ... ."

"Blood and guts?"

Maddie snorted. "That didn't really bother me," she said. "It was more that I couldn't take the sadness. It was great when we saved someone and they had a happy outcome. When someone died, though, that's what I couldn't take."

"You always were sensitive," Todd said. "I remember you adopting stray animals every chance you got."

"I've always liked animals."

"And your mom just let you bring them home?"

"She liked animals, too."

"Did you come home because your mom died?" Todd asked.

"Partially," Maddie said. "Someone needs to take care of Granny."

"Yeah, she's a real spitfire," Todd said, chuckling. "I especially like how she's always going after Harriet Proctor. Those two are like oil and vinegar."

"They've hated each other since they were kids," Maddie said. "That's what Granny says, anyway. She claims Harriet tried to steal my grandfather from her."

"That's a frightening picture," Todd said. "You said you partially came home because of your mother's death. Why else?"

"I just wanted to come home," Maddie said. "I don't think city life was for me. Someone needs to run the shop. I've always loved that shop, so it seemed like a natural fit."

"Well, the city's loss is my incredible gain," Todd said, reaching across the table and wrapping his hand around Maddie's wrist. "Let's decide what we want to order. Did I mention how good the lobster is?"

NICK WAS IN A HORRIBLE MOOD. He'd had every intention of leaving work, crawling into bed, and forgetting all about his day. That wasn't in the cards.

He'd found Cassidy sitting on his front porch, a bright smile and a nice dress illuminating her pretty features, when he got home. He'd never given her a key – he didn't like people in his personal space – so she'd been forced to sit on his porch for more than an hour.

When she'd suggested a nice dinner out, Nick balked. Not only did he not want to go out to dinner, he also didn't want to spend any time with Cassidy. He had no idea why, but her very existence was starting to grate on him.

She was always so nice and friendly. She was never in a bad mood. She never tried to force him into things he didn't want to do. There was absolutely nothing wrong with her. "Except she's not Maddie," a voice whispered in the back of his mind.

It wasn't the first time he'd heard the voice. It had reared its ugly head every time he dated a woman over the past decade. He'd learned to ignore it. It was easy when Maddie wasn't there. Now that she was back, it was darned near impossible. Nick knew he was at a crossroads. He just had to pick a direction, and the one he was leaning toward was going to devastate Cassidy.

So, he'd agreed to dinner. She wanted a nice night out. She wanted seafood and a view. He could give her that. For now.

"We haven't been here since our first date," Cassidy enthused, her eyes shining as the hostess led them across the dining room. "I'm so excited."

"I'm glad," Nick said.

"Aren't you excited?"

"Sure."

"Will this table work?"

Nick smiled at the hostess. "It's fine."

"Oh, do you have something by a window?" Cassidy asked hopefully.

"I'm sorry," the hostess said. "They got the last one."

Nick lifted his head to stare at the couple the hostess was referring to and pulled up short. The sight of Maddie sitting there – he didn't even recognize her at first – was enough to throw him. The realization of her date's identity as he held her hand across the table felt like a semi-truck rolling over him.

"Todd."

MADDIE FELT like she was caught in a trap. It was bad enough she was stuck on an uncomfortable date in an outfit that left little to the imagination, but Nick's arrival was creating enough pressure on her chest to virtually smother her.

"Oh, hi," Cassidy said, her voice bright.

"Hi," Maddie replied dully.

"Winters." Todd's tone was terse.

"Winthrop." Nick's tone was deadly.

"Oh, do you two know each other?" Cassidy asked, oblivious.

"We all went to high school together," Maddie explained.

"Oh, that's great," Cassidy said. "We can all sit together and catch up. Our lunch the other day got cut short. We really wanted to sit at a window anyway." She turned to the hostess. "Can we just sit with them?"

The hostess shrugged. "Knock yourself out."

"I don't think … ." Nick broke off, unsure.

"Yeah, we're on our first date," Todd said. "That's not really a group activity. I'm not going to be able to flirt with her if I have an audience."

Nick narrowed his eyes as he regarded Maddie. "You know what? It sounds like fun." He took the open seat between Maddie and Todd and plopped down in it. He reached over and snagged one of the menus from the hostess. "Have you ordered yet?"

"We were just about to," Maddie said.

"Winters, do I infringe on your dates?" Todd asked.

"Sit down, Cassidy," Nick ordered. "I left the seat right by the window open for you."

Maddie glanced at Cassidy and found the girl's face hard to fathom. It was a blank slate, but there was something there lurking in the depths of her eyes. After a moment, Cassidy plastered an obviously fake smile on her face and settled in the chair Nick had indicated.

"I really love this place," she said. "Oh, I'm Cassidy, by the way." She extended her hand in Todd's direction.

"Todd Winthrop."

"And you all went to high school together?"

"Yup," Nick said.

"Did you all hang out?" Either Cassidy was oblivious or she was purposely leading the conversation into the middle of a minefield. Maddie wasn't sure which one was true. Since her heart was beating so rapidly, she was having trouble hearing anything else that was going on, though.

"No, we didn't exactly run in the same circles," Todd said.

"Oh, what circle did you run in?"

"I was with the popular group," Todd said. "These two were ... their own little group."

Cassidy swallowed hard. "Yes, I've heard they were ... tight."

Todd barked out a laugh. "Tight? They were inseparable. You never saw one without the other. I think Winters here would've followed Maddie into the bathroom if he could have. He was a little protective of her."

"You were protective of her?" Cassidy asked, shifting her attention to Nick. "Did she need protection?"

"I wasn't protective of her," Nick said. "Todd just didn't understand that no means no."

Cassidy faltered. "I don't understand."

"Oh, well, it's just that Todd was always sniffing around Maddie and asking her out – even though he knew she wasn't interested," Nick said. "She had good taste ... at least she did when we were younger."

"I'll bet you had to beat the boys off with a stick when you were in high school," Cassidy said, her eyes practically begging Maddie to intervene.

"Not really," Maddie said.

"Yeah, I couldn't find a stick big enough to beat Todd off with," Nick said. Maddie pursed her lips to keep from laughing at the awkward statement. Nick shot her a look. "You know what I mean."

"So, you had a crush on Maddie in high school?" Cassidy asked, gripping her glass nervously.

"Everyone had a crush on Maddie," Todd said, his smile lazy. "She only had eyes for Nick here, though. Everyone thought they were going to get married."

"But, they didn't," Cassidy said.

"Nope, they certainly didn't," Todd said. "Instead, Maddie dumped him in the dirt and left him a broken man."

Maddie leaned forward, angry. "That is not what happened."

Todd shushed Maddie. "Winters and I are in the middle of a conversation, sweetheart. Drink your Diet Coke."

"Don't talk to her that way," Nick warned.

"What way was I talking to her?"

"Like she was your … property," Nick said. "Show her some respect."

"Like you're showing your date?" Todd pressed. "Have you even noticed that she's sitting at the same table? You seem a lot more interested in your good *friend* Maddie than your actual date."

Nick scowled. "Maybe I just don't like Maddie falling victim to your … crap," Nick shot back. He turned to Maddie. "Do you know how many women this guy goes through every month?"

"I … ."

"How could you even agree to go out with him?" Nick asked, incensed.

"I didn't give her an option to say no," Todd replied. "I asked her if she was involved with someone. She said she wasn't. I told her we were coming to dinner, and here we are."

"Wow, you're so romantic," Nick deadpanned.

"Maybe sitting at the same table was a bad idea," Cassidy interjected.

Maddie couldn't help but agree with her. "You know, I'm not feeling very well. As fun as this evening has been – and it has been fun – I really think we should cut it short."

"You haven't even ordered yet," Todd said, brushing off her statement. "I haven't even had a chance to ply you with alcohol so I can take advantage of you later."

Nick slammed his hand down on the table. "Stop it."

"You stop it," Todd said. "You're the one who cut in on my date. In case you haven't noticed, she's not your personal plaything anymore, Winters. She's open for offers, and I'm offering."

"No, you're not," Nick said, getting to his feet. "Come on, Maddie. I'm taking you home."

"You can't do that," Todd said. "I brought her here. You can't take her home."

"Yes, I can," Nick seethed.

"No, you can't," Cassidy chimed in. "In case you forgot, we came in your truck. There's only room for two of us."

"Well, then Todd can take you home, Cassidy," Nick sputtered. "I'll take Maddie home."

Cassidy reared back as if she'd been smacked. Maddie's heart went out to her. "Nick," she hissed. "You can't do this."

Nick growled. "I … ."

"Nicky," Maddie's voice was low and full of warning. "What you're doing is so … wrong."

"Let's go, Cassidy," Nick said, letting go of Maddie's wrist and straightening. He was resigned. "I think I've lost my appetite."

10. TEN

"That is horrible," Christy chortled, leaning back in the chair next to the tarot table and hanging her head. "That's like the worst date ever."

"I was hoping it was just a nightmare," Maddie admitted, topping off Christy's mug of coffee and then replacing the pot on the warming burner on the counter. "Unfortunately, I woke up and saw the dress you loaned me hanging on the chair and knew it had all really happened."

Christy had appeared at the front door of Magicks first thing the following morning, dying for some scoop. She had no idea just how much "scoop" she was going to get.

"So, how did the evening end?"

"Well, Nick and Cassidy left, and Todd insisted I order the lobster."

"You don't like lobster?"

Maddie shrugged. "I'm happy with a cheeseburger and fries."

"Girl, we are going to have to give you a food and clothing makeover," Christy said. "How did Todd act after Nick left?"

"Like he'd won the lottery."

Christy furrowed her brow. "What do you mean?"

"I don't think Todd even likes me," Maddie said. "I just think he wants to beat Nick. Although, I have no idea what he thinks he's beating Nick at."

"You're such an idiot," Christy said.

"Excuse me?"

"Nick is in love with you, Maddie," Christy said. "Tell me you don't know that."

"He's not in love with me," Maddie scoffed. "He's really angry with me. You should've seen him last night."

"Maddie, think about the scene you described to me," Christy said, forcing her voice to remain even. "Nick ignored Cassidy, and he focused on you and Todd. He picked a fight with Todd, and then insisted on taking you home. When Cassidy pointed out there wasn't enough room in the truck, he suggested Todd take her home. He didn't show any concern for Cassidy at all. He only cared about what happened with you."

"That's just because he wanted to beat Todd."

"Yeah, maybe part of him wanted to beat Todd," Christy conceded. "It wasn't just about beating Todd, though. It was about winning the prize – and that prize was you."

"You don't know what you're saying," Maddie said, turning to face the shelf behind the counter so Christy couldn't see her expression. "Nick is in a relationship."

"With a woman he doesn't really care about," Christy said. "Listen, I know you think Nick walks on water, but he's not exactly infallible."

"What is that supposed to mean?"

"He's never treated Cassidy poorly," Christy said. "He's never treated any of the women he's dated poorly. He's just never really ... engaged with them."

When Maddie turned back around, she was trying to hide her interest. "What do you mean?"

Christy smirked. "Nick was the kind of guy who would date a woman for exactly six months, and then find a reason to dump her," Christy said. "You could time it like clockwork. He never gave them keys to his house. I'm fairly certain he never even let them spend the night at his house.

"He was polite, and he was respectful, but he was never emotionally engaged," she continued. "He just wasn't interested in forever with anyone."

Maddie nodded.

"Except you," Christy added.

Maddie's eyebrows jumped. "Except I never dated Nick."

"What do you think all those outings to Willow Lake were?"

"We were just ... hanging out."

"Uh-huh." Christy didn't look convinced. "Did you ever hold hands?"

"What? No!"

"Never?"

"Only when we were going through the woods at night," Maddie corrected. "He didn't want me to trip."

"Did you ever, I don't know, touch each other?"

"Define touch."

"Not like that," Christy said, laughing. "I'm asking if he ever put his arms around you, if he ever held your head when you were resting it on his chest on those nights when you were out in the field looking at the stars, if he ever kissed your forehead when you were just sitting together."

"How did you know about that?"

"Aha! I didn't," Christy replied, excited. "That's just how I always pictured it. I knew you were holding out on me."

"That was just friendly stuff," Maddie protested.

"No, it wasn't," Christy said, flicking Maddie on the arm. "That's friendly stuff. We're friends. You and Nick are so much more than that."

"We haven't seen each other in ten years."

"Sometimes love transcends time," Christy said. "That's the kind of love you share with Nick. You both just need to accept it."

Maddie bit her bottom lip. "He doesn't love me."

"Yes, he does," Christy said. "You're just not ready to let him. It's okay. You have time. You have all the time in the world, Maddie. Cassidy's six-month lease is about to expire. Just ... think about it."

MADDIE DIDN'T WANT to think about Christy's words. She wanted to think about something else – anything else, really. If she dwelled on them, something foreign invaded her soul: Hope.

She couldn't have hope. She was a freak. Nick could never be with a freak. He deserved a normal life. He deserved a normal wife. He deserved normal kids, a normal home, a normal ... everything. Nothing about Maddie was normal. She wasn't what Nick deserved.

When the walls of Magicks started closing in on her heavy thoughts, Maddie escaped to the woods behind the house. She hadn't spent nearly enough time out there since her return. When she was younger, she wasted hours getting lost in the woods searching for mushrooms, and in the meadow picking flowers, and at Willow Lake just ... exploring.

That's exactly what she wanted to do now.

When she got to the lake, Maddie kicked her sneakers off and tossed them under a nearby tree. After removing her socks, Maddie rolled up her Capri pants and waded into the cool water.

Once summer was in full swing, and the humidity hit like a heat-seeking missile, the water would be a welcome respite. Now it was cold enough to jolt her and send the blood coursing through her body. It was invigorating.

Maddie splashed her feet through the water, smiling when she saw a turtle poke its head out of the shallows and glare in her direction. She'd always loved the turtles. They were so cute ... and grumpy. They reminded her of Maude.

Maddie jolted backward when a figure moved into her line of sight and snatched the turtle out of the water with quick hands. Nick smiled at her as he cradled the turtle to his chest. "Some things never change."

"No, they don't," Maddie said, returning the smile as she fought to catch her breath. Even though their evening the night before had been straight out of a nightmare, something about the familiar setting erased all of the harsh words and recriminations. "Did you catch that for me?"

Nick grinned. "Don't I always?"

He handed her the turtle, watching as it struggled in her hands as she gripped it tightly.

"How did you know I was down here?"

"I just had a feeling," Nick said. He bent down to unlace his own shoes and socks and then rolled up his jeans before stepping into the water. He was out of uniform, so Maddie figured he was off duty. "You always come down here when you have something you want to think about. I figured last night definitely fell into that category. Wow. This is cold."

"It's early in the season," Maddie said, bending over and releasing the turtle. "Farewell, Monty."

Nick barked out a laugh. "Are you still naming them before you release them?"

"I guess so. It's been ten years since I've had one to release."

"Ah, Freddy," Nick said, nodding knowingly. "He was one of a kind. It took me twenty minutes to catch him."

Maddie was flabbergasted. "You remember that?"

"I remember it all," Nick said, exhaling heavily. "I remember it all."

"Me, too," Maddie said. "I also remember you having something of a meltdown last night."

"Yeah, that's why I came looking for you," Nick said. "I owe you an apology."

"No, you don't, Nicky," Maddie said. "You actually saved me."

"I did?" Nick raised his dark eyebrows, surprised.

"It was a horrible night before you got there," Maddie admitted. "It only got worse once you left."

"Why? Did he put his hands on you?"

Maddie was taken aback by Nick's vehemence. "No. He tried to force feed me lobster, and then he tried to make me go for a walk with him on the beach, and then he brought me home."

"Did he ... did he kiss you?"

"Do you really want to know the answer to that?"

"No," Nick said. "Did he?"

Maddie snickered. "No. Maude was waiting on the front porch. She threatened him with a potato chip bag clip to the groin if he put the moves on me."

"I've always loved Maude."

"She's always loved you." Maddie bent over to study the ground by her feet, plunging her hand into the water and returning with a stone. She rubbed it, studied it for a second, and then tossed it to Nick. "For luck."

Nick caught the rock. "It's a Petoskey Stone."

"They're still your favorite, aren't they?"

"I love Petoskey Stones like you love turtles," Nick said. He stuck the stone in his pocket. "I really am sorry about what happened last night."

"It was a horrible situation," Maddie said. "I still don't know how I ended up there – especially in that dress."

"Yeah, that was something new," Nick said. "I didn't even know you owned a dress like that."

"Christy and Maude forced me into it," Maddie said. "They're not big on boundaries. I told them it wasn't me, but they just don't listen sometimes."

"You looked beautiful in the dress, Mad," Nick said. "You just shouldn't have worn it for the likes of Todd Winthrop."

Maddie had no idea why she pushed the subject, but she couldn't stop herself. "Who should I have worn it for?"

Nick pursed his lips. "I don't know," he said finally. "Who did you want to wear it for?"

"I never wanted to wear that dress for anyone," Maddie said. "I felt like I was naked. It was too small for me."

"The dress was not too small for you," Nick said. "You looked like ... an angel. A really ... hot ... angel."

Maddie snorted as her cheeks warmed. "You don't have to lie to me. I know I looked ridiculous."

"Maddie ... I wish you would stop doing that," Nick said.

"What?"

"You don't see yourself how others see you," he said. "You never have. That's your biggest fault. You don't see how ... beautiful you are. You see the beauty in others fine. When you look at yourself, though, you see something else. I've always wondered what that is."

"I just see ... me," Maddie said. "Just plain, old Maddie."

"You're such a putz."

Maddie kicked out with her foot and splashed him. "You're a putz."

Nick extended his finger. "Don't start a war you can't win, missy."

"Who says I can't win?"

Nick bent over and cupped his hands in the water, aiming them at Maddie.

"Don't you dare!"

"Say you can't win."

"No."

"Say you can't win," Nick pressed.

"No."

Nick scooped the water up and flung it in Maddie's direction, leaving her drenched. Maddie's mouth dropped open as she pushed her stringy hair out of her face. "I can't believe you did that."

"You wouldn't admit my water superiority," Nick said.

Maddie whipped her hands through the water and coated Nick with a cold layer before he could move away.

"Holy crap! That is cold," Nick said. "Oh, and you're going to pay now." He slogged through the water. Since his legs were longer, even though Maddie tried to flee, he caught up with her quickly, grabbing her around the waist and twirling her around. "I'm going to have to dunk you now."

"No, you can't," Maddie gasped, her heart racing as his body pressed close to hers. Even though she was freezing, she suddenly couldn't focus on anything but the warmth his body offered. "I'll get sick if you dunk me."

Nick's face softened. "Tell me what I want to hear."

Maddie made an exasperated sound in the back of her throat. "Fine. You're the king."

Nick smiled.

"Of putzes," Maddie grumbled.

Nick flicked the end of her nose. "We need to get out of this water before one of us really does get sick." He gripped Maddie's hand as he pulled away. She missed his warmth instantaneously, but the feeling of his fingers as they linked with hers was a new sensation to grapple with.

Once they were on the grassy embankment and settled on the ground, Maddie instinctively leaned over and rested her head against his shoulder. She'd done it so many times before, it didn't seem like a strange move. Nick returned the gesture, resting his cheek against her head. "Oh, my Maddie," he said. "I know I haven't told you this yet, but I'm really glad you came home."

"Me, too."

"I'm still mad at you."

"I know."

"I'm glad you're here, though."

"Me, too," Maddie said, sighing. She searched her mind for a topic to continue the conversation. She didn't want to pull away from him. She needed to think of something to converse about. "So, do you know who killed Sarah Alden yet?"

Nick's body stiffened. "We haven't released her name yet. How do you know it?"

Maddie's heart sank into her stomach. *Oh no.*

11. ELEVEN

Nick leaned back in his office desk chair and studied the ceiling. Blackstone Bay was a small department. There were only three full-time officers, and even though the building was small, there was more than enough room for everyone to be able to spread out. That was a welcome thing – especially today. He couldn't deal with … people.

Technically, he was off duty. Kreskin was handling Sarah Alden's death, and Nick's biggest problem today was supposed to be avoiding Cassidy. Life had interrupted. Again.

Nick rubbed his forehead, weary. He was at a loss with Cassidy. He had nothing against her, but he wasn't exactly emotionally invested in her either. In fact, he'd been preparing just how he was going to break up with her when his world tilted. He'd known she wasn't the one for him after the first date. That didn't mean she wasn't fun and easy to handle. As long as she didn't make demands, Nick was happy to let the relationship float in the ether. It was never going to move to the next step. Maddie's return hadn't changed that.

Now? Now Nick knew that any decision he made was going to be blamed on Maddie. Before she returned, the town would've chalked up the breakup to Nick's six-month cycle. He was well aware of the whispers. He'd argued against them a few times, only ceasing when he realized they were true. Things were different now.

Now *his* Maddie was home.

Nick had known from the second he saw her that all the love he'd long since forgotten – and stuffed away – was still there. He'd tried to convince himself he was over her, but it wasn't true. He was never going to be over her. He was never going to be able to move beyond her. He was never going to be able to let her go.

That didn't mean they had a future. That's what Nick had to keep reminding himself. Maddie had never once insinuated that she had feelings for him. Oh, sure, she loved him – but it was just as a friend. Now, Nick had a question to ask himself: Was friendship enough?

The truth was, he had no idea. He couldn't focus on that right now. He had other things to ponder. First off? How had Maddie known Sarah Alden's name?

She claimed she'd heard it whispered in town, but when Nick questioned from where, she'd clammed up. Her answers had been vague, her memory suddenly faulty. From the woman who remembered the last turtle they'd snared together, Nick had his doubts. She was hiding something. He just didn't know what.

Nick stilled, his fingers poised over his computer keyboard. What he was about to do was a gross invasion of privacy. He was an ethical man, and yet he couldn't stop himself. He typed her name into the search engine.

He pressed his eyes together briefly when the information popped up on the screen, and then he tamped down his reservations. He had to know what she was hiding. If it was something they could overcome … .

Nick sighed and focused on the screen. There was a lot to search through. Why would she have so much activity in a police database?

Nick clicked on the oldest file and read the report from Officer Dwight Kincaid. He was with the Detroit Police Department and had since been promoted to detective. His notes were terse and hard to decipher, but he mentioned solving a hit-and-run with the help of a nurse at a local hospital. The report didn't go into detail, and Nick was more lost when he was done reading than he had been when he started.

Nick clicked on the next file, and then the next, and then the next. He wasted three hours going through the files. Maddie was listed as a consultant in each and every one.

"Maddie," Nick muttered. "How?"

Nick rolled his neck, an audible "crack" filling the room. There wasn't enough in the files to give him something to go on. He had to dig further. He had to … know. Nick reached for the phone on his desk and punched in the number in the files. He waited for someone to pick up.

"Detective Kincaid."

Nick sucked in a breath. Part of him hadn't expected the man to answer. "Um, hi. My name is Nick Winters. I'm a detective with the Blackstone Bay Police Department."

"Isn't that up by Traverse City?"

"Yeah."

"That's a beautiful area," Kincaid said. "What can I do to help you?"

"I … um … this is going to sound weird," Nick said, unsure.

"I live in Detroit," Kincaid said. "Everything in this city is weird."

Nick hadn't really thought about how he was going to broach the subject of Maddie's appearance in the files before he made the call. Now he had no choice but to make up a lie on the fly. "We had a homicide here the other day," he said. "A local woman found the body. Well, she used to be a local woman, and she just moved back to the area, so I guess she's local again … ."

"I have a lot of files on my desk to clear before I leave for the day," Kincaid said. "Can you get to the point?"

Nick pursed his lips. "We're just doing some routine checks," he said. "When I ran the woman who found the body through our search engines, I found her in a lot of your files."

"Who are we talking about?"

"Maddie … Madeline … Graves."

Nick heard the detective suck in a breath. "Is she in trouble?"

"So, you do know her?"

"I know her," Kincaid said. "Is she in trouble?"

"Are you asking if she's a suspect in the murder?"

"I'm asking if she's in trouble," Kincaid said. "I can be up there in … two days … if she is. You can't question her without an attorney."

Nick was floored. *Since when does a cop tell another cop not to question a suspect?* "She's not a suspect," Nick said. "I just want to know why she's in so many of your files."

"She helped with some cases," Kincaid said. "She's a good woman. She wouldn't kill anyone."

"I know she's a good woman," Nick snapped. "I want to know how you know she's a good woman."

"I'm sorry, can you clarify what's going on here?"

Nick had nothing to lose. "I've known Maddie since we were kids. She's been back in town for less than a week, and she discovered a dead body. She's acting … odd. I need to know how to protect her."

Silence.

"Are you still there?"

"What did you say your name was again?" Kincaid asked.

"Nick Winters."

"You're the best friend," Kincaid said.

Nick sucked in a breath. "Who told you that?"

"She did," Kincaid said. "Listen, I know how close you two were … are … were. Whatever. I want you to tell me why you're really calling."

"Maddie is hiding something," Nick said. "She knew the name of a murder victim before it was released to the public. Suspicion is going to fall on her."

"She wouldn't kill anyone," Kincaid said. "She's not capable of it."

The detective's matter-of-fact tone was enough to tip Nick over the edge. "I know she's not capable of it. I've known that since she went around saving ants from the little shits we went to elementary school with. They were vicious with their magnifying glasses. I want to know how she helped you with these cases."

"Ask her."

"She won't tell me," Nick said, frustrated. "She's … hiding."

Kincaid sighed. "Listen, I probably know more about your relationship with Maddie than I have any business knowing," he said. "I know that you're her ... frickin' soul mate ... if that's really a thing. I also know that she's a private person, and she's struggling with an obnoxious amount of crap."

Nick cleared his throat. "How did Maddie help you?"

"She worked as an independent consultant."

"Doing what?"

"She was ... she was kind of the psychic our department utilized for missing person cases."

Nick swallowed hard. "I'm sorry, you're going to need to ... she was ... how was she a psychic?"

"Oh, boy, I can tell you're in a state," Kincaid said. "I can't betray her."

"I'm not asking you to betray her."

"I made a promise," Kincaid said. "I don't know if that means anything to you, but it means something to me. All I can say is that she was ... invaluable ... to some of our investigations. She found more than twenty people. That last thing was ... unfortunate."

"What last thing?" Nick was desperate.

"That's her story to tell," Kincaid said.

"But ... ."

"Detective Winters, I know you and Maddie have a history," Kincaid said. "I know because every time she mentioned you her face lit up. It was the only time I ever saw her smile. She was a ... sad little thing."

Nick's heart pinged.

"She was also a brave little thing," Kincaid said. "When you see her ... when you talk to her about this ... make sure she knows what happened wasn't her fault. She did the best she could."

Nick was lost. "I don't know what you're talking about."

"Give her time," Kincaid said. "If anyone can get her to open up, I have a feeling it's you."

"I need to take care of her," Nick said. "She ... her mother just died."

Kincaid sighed. "I'm sorry to hear that," he said. "I know she didn't have a lot of family. From what I understand, all she had was a grandmother, the mother, and ... you. Are you still her family?"

Nick swallowed the painful lump in his throat. "I'll always be her family."

"Then give her time ... and space," Kincaid said. "She'll talk when she's ready."

Nick wasn't sure he could do that.

12. TWELVE

Blackstone Bay's spring festival was a welcome memory from the past. As Maddie walked through the fair, a bag of cotton candy clutched in her hand, she couldn't help but be reminded of fun times. Of course, all those memories revolved around Nick.

They'd come to the fair together every year. Nick had insisted on winning her a stuffed animal, she had a whole collection, and they'd spent hours in the funhouse before gorging themselves on elephant ears and ice cream. This experience was ... different.

"So, what did you do today?" Christy asked, popping into view out of nowhere.

Maddie jerked back. "I'm going to get you a bell to wear around your neck."

"My neck is too fat for a choker."

"You're not fat."

"I'm not thin either," Christy pointed out.

"Who cares about stuff like that?" Maddie said, offering the effervescent redhead a hunk of cotton candy. "As long as you're happy, that's all that matters."

Christy took the spun fluff. "How was your afternoon?"

"Fine," Maddie said, forcing the memory of Nick and the lake out of her mind. "Why? How was your afternoon?"

"I cut hair," Christy said. "Oh, and I foiled Agnes Milkens. She's convinced she can't find a man because she doesn't have highlights."

"Isn't Agnes ninety?"

"She's still on the prowl," Christy said. "What about you? Did you have fun with Nick down at the lake?"

Maddie was stunned. "Who told you about that?"

"Ha!" Christy poked Maddie in the chest. "You just did. What did you two do?"

"You need to stop tricking me," Maddie said, annoyed. "That's not playing fair."

"Life isn't fair," Christy said. "So, spill. What did you and Nick do down at the lake?"

"He caught a turtle for me."

"And?"

"And we splashed water on each other."

"And?"

"And then nothing," Maddie said. "He had to get to work."

"You're a bad liar," Christy said, grabbing Maddie's bag of cotton candy from her irritably. "But, since I'm such a good person, I'm going to let this go. You're still fighting the Nick Effect."

"What's the Nick Effect?"

"Oh, that's that low-down tingle you feel in your loins every time you see him," Christy said, ignoring the flush moving up Maddie's neck and cheeks. "How about we go on a ride?"

"I don't really like rides," Maddie said. "I have a weak stomach."

"You'll like rides if I give you one."

Maddie froze when she heard the voice. It had been less than twenty-four hours since Todd had dropped her off, but she was hoping it would be at least another twenty-four years before she saw him again.

"Oh, Todd," Christy said, looking him up and down. "You're looking ... smarmy."

"Christy," Todd said, his tone dismissive. "Isn't there some hair you should be cutting?"

"Nope. I'm off for the night."

"What are you doing here?" Maddie asked, uncomfortable.

"It's the town fair," Todd said. "Everyone comes. I called you earlier today, by the way. You didn't call me back."

"I was busy," Maddie lied. "I've been working fifteen hours a day to get Magicks back up and into working order."

Todd was nonplussed. "You couldn't spare five minutes?"

"I . . . ."

"She was with me," Christy interjected. "We were doing girl stuff."

"What's girl stuff?"

"You know, makeup and hair stuff."

"I guess I don't know," Todd said. "I'm not a girl."

"Oh, that's not the word on the street," Christy said.

Maddie's mouth dropped open. "Christy," she hissed.

Todd narrowed his eyes. "Well, since you two spent the afternoon together, I'm guessing you don't need to spend the night together," he said. He held out his hand to Maddie. "How about we go on a few rides?"

Maddie was immediately shaking her head. "Oh, I'm sorry," she said. "Christy and I have plans."

Christy nodded.

"Plans to do what?"

"We're having a girls' night," Christy said. "No men allowed."

Todd straightened and scanned the crowd. "No men? Or just not this man?"

"All men," Maddie said, her face apologetic. "Sorry. Maybe some other time."

NICK USED to love a good fair. He'd spend hours – days even – frequenting each and every one. Maddie loved the flea markets. She'd buy ugly little craft items and shove them in her purse to peruse later. They'd ride the swings together, her stomach couldn't take much more than that, and then she'd watch him play games for hours.

Tonight Nick couldn't stand the fair. Cassidy had insisted they attend, and Nick was still fighting the urge to drop her. If he did it now, Marla and her minions would peck Maddie to death. That was an added problem Nick just couldn't deal with right now.

"Do you want to get something to eat?" Cassidy asked hopefully.

"I'm not really hungry."

"How about … we could go to the funhouse?"

Nick stilled. He hadn't been in a funhouse since … since the night Maddie had screamed when the murderous clown jumped out of the corner. She'd thrown herself into his arms for protection. He loved that memory. He could still smell the flowery scent of her shampoo. "I don't like funhouses."

"Okay," Cassidy said, searching for options. "There's a band over at the square."

"Fine," Nick said. "Let's go listen to the band."

Cassidy reached over and grabbed his hand, her face falling when he snatched it away and ran it through his hair.

"We should go now," Nick said. "I have to be up early tomorrow. I only have an hour to burn."

"Right," Cassidy said. "You have work tomorrow."

"I have work every day," Nick said. "We're dealing with a murder." He was also dealing with thoughts of Maddie – and Detective Kincaid – but he couldn't talk about that.

"I know," Cassidy said. "I … we should listen to the band."

The town square was packed when they arrived. Nick bought two beers at the concession stand and gave one to Cassidy before he settled at a busy picnic table. He'd purposely picked one where there wasn't an open spot at his side. After scanning the table dejectedly, Cassidy opted to sit across from him.

"So, any idea who killed that lady the other day?" Pete Harper asked.

"Nope," Nick said, swigging from his beer. "I'm not in charge of the case."

"I heard Maddie Graves found her," Tom Peters said.

"I've seen her around town," Kevin Milligan said. "She looks ... hot."

"She does look hot," Pete said. "She was always hot, but she's downright smoking now."

"Have you seen her since she's been back?" Tom asked, turning to Nick.

"I have," Nick said. "I was at the scene yesterday."

"You two were always a sight to behold," Kevin said. "I was always jealous. I was two years older than you guys, but Maddie was so beautiful I was willing to be held back."

"She is beautiful," Nick agreed, forcing his gaze to remain steady on the band as they caroused on the stage.

"Are you two going to pick up where you left off?" Tom asked.

Nick swallowed a gulp of beer, risking a quick glance at Cassidy to see how she was handling the conversation. For her part, she was pretending to be entranced with the show. Nick knew better. "We were friends," he said. "Nothing else."

"Oh, please," Kevin said. "You two were so hot for each other you could've set the world on fire."

"We were friends," Nick repeated, forcing his eyes to scan the crowd congregating near the concession stand. When his gaze landed on bright blonde hair, his heart skipped a beat. "We were just friends."

"Right," Tom said, rolling his eyes.

Nick watched Maddie and Christy as they chatted. Maddie's heart-shaped face was animated, and whatever story Christy was telling had her laughing out loud. That was the first time he'd seen it since she returned. It was a genuine smile and a genuine laugh. It was ... breathtaking.

The conversation at the picnic table continued without his input, and Nick let his mind wander as he watched Maddie. Christy bought an elephant ear, and she split it down the middle so the two women could share it.

She looked happy, Nick mused. Well, she looked happier. He'd yet to see her look truly happy. What would that be like? He couldn't help but imagine Heaven.

Suddenly, Maddie bent over at the waist and grabbed her stomach. Christy's face was ashen as she leaned down and pushed Maddie's blonde hair out of the way. Nick couldn't read lips, but he knew concern when he saw it.

"Where are you going?" Cassidy asked.

Nick ignored her as he increased his pace and headed toward Maddie. She needed him.

SOMETHING WAS WRONG. Maddie's stomach was twisted – and that could only mean one thing: Someone was in trouble.

"Maddie, what's wrong?" Christy asked. "Is it the elephant ear? Are you going to be sick?"

Maddie fought to control her breathing. "I … ."

"Maddie!" Nick was at her side, his hand on her hip before she could get her bearings. "What's wrong?"

"I think she's sick," Christy said. "She was fine a second ago."

Nick rubbed Maddie's back. "Let's get away from the crowd," he said. "You probably just need to sit down."

"There's a spot over there," Christy said, pointing.

"Uh, yeah, I've got her," Nick said, wrapping his arm around Maddie's waist. "Why don't you go and watch the band? I'll take care of her. We'll be back over there in a few minutes."

"Okay," Christy said brightly, her gaze bouncing between the two of them. "Have fun."

If he wasn't so worried about Maddie, Nick would've wondered why Christy left without an argument. He'd known her long enough to realize that unquestionable retreat wasn't in her repertoire. Nick was too thankful for her easy exit to question it.

Nick led Maddie to the far side of the square, watching as she leaned against a brick wall and rubbed her forehead. "Did you eat something bad?"

"Well, I've eaten cotton candy, a corn dog, and an elephant ear," Maddie said, her smile rueful. "I haven't eaten anything good."

"You always did like junk," Nick said, massaging her neck. "You're really pale, love."

Maddie pressed her eyes shut, the term of endearment filling her with warmth. "I'm just … oh." Maddie grabbed her stomach again.

"If you're going to throw up, let's move farther away," Nick prodded. "I know you don't want anyone to see you puke."

"I … we have to go this way," Maddie said, gasping as she grabbed Nick's hand. "This way."

Nick was confused, but he followed. Maddie's path was winding, and she stopped every few seconds to get her bearings. She didn't sit down, though, no matter how many times Nick prodded her to do just that.

Before he realized what was happening, Nick found himself two blocks away from the fair. Maddie's face was red from exertion, but he didn't stop her. Finally, after turning one more corner and arriving in the pharmacy parking lot, Maddie managed to straighten her frame. She extended her arm and pointed to the lone car. "There."

Nick was confused. "What's there?"

"There," Maddie said, her voice breaking as she shook her arm. "There."

Nick moved in the direction she was pointing. He didn't want to leave her, but she was insistent. The closer he got to the car, the more agitated he was. Then he heard it … the small sound of sobs. Someone was on the other side of the car.

Nick increased his pace and rounded the vehicle, pulling up short when he saw the small child sitting on the pavement, knees pulled to her chest.

"Sadie?"

He recognized the girl. Mary Thompson had four kids, and Sadie was the youngest. Nick didn't like to judge people, but Mary was hardly an observant mother. "Sadie? Are you okay?"

Sadie lifted her tear-streaked face. "I'm losted."

"You're not lost," Nick said, reaching down and pulling her to her feet. "You're just … misplaced."

"I'm tired," Sadie wailed. "I want to go home."

"Where is your mother?" Nick asked, glancing over his shoulder so he could study Maddie. She looked markedly better. She was standing up straight, her shoulders squared, and the color was returning to her cheeks. "Is she at the fair?"

"She wouldn't let me go on the ride," Sadie said. "I ran away. I thought she would find me."

"You're a long way from the fair, Sadie," Nick said, clasping his hand around the girl's small wrist. "I'm going to take you back to your mommy."

"Good," Sadie said, jutting her lip out. "I want some cotton candy."

Nick nodded. "I'll buy you some." He led Sadie over to where Maddie was standing. "How did you know she was here?"

Maddie balked. "I … I was just sick. I didn't know she was here."

"Right," Nick said, his conversation with Kincaid rushing through his mind. "Right."

Something here was wrong. Something here was very wrong with Maddie. Nick just couldn't figure out what.

13. THIRTEEN

Magicks was officially open. Again.

There was no fanfare. There was no ribbon cutting. There was no party. It was just ... a normal day. Maddie loved normal days. She could count the number of normal days she'd ever experienced on one hand. She wanted a normal day – even if it meant no customers would cross the threshold.

"This place is deader than a senior citizen wedding," Maude announced.

Maddie looked up from the tarot table where she was reading a book and scowled. "Why are you even here?"

"Listen, pain in my ass, I'm your only customer right now," Maude said, rolling her eyes. "You shouldn't burn your bridges."

"I'm not burning my bridges," Maddie scoffed. "I'm ... ."

Maude snickered. "Girl, you are a mess."

Maddie rubbed her forehead ruefully.

"I happen to like a mess," Maude said, settling in the chair on the opposite side of the table and fixing Maddie with an inquisitive look. "What have you been up to?"

"Nothing."

Maude arched an eyebrow.

"What have you heard?" Maddie was flustered.

"I heard you found a missing child last night," Maude said. "The whole town is buzzing about it."

Maddie's face fell. "Oh no."

"Maddie, you have to let this ... shame ... go," Maude said. "You have nothing to be embarrassed about."

"Who says I'm embarrassed?"

"That red face of yours," Maude said. "If you hadn't stepped in, Sadie might have wandered farther away. What if a pervert had found her? Speaking of, did you see Todd?"

Maddie scowled. "I saw him. I can't shake him. I blame you."

"I'll kill him if you want me to," Maude said. "We can dump the body in the woods."

"You're not funny."

"I'm not trying to be funny," Maude said. "I'm trying to be practical. Everyone in this county knows that Todd Winthrop is an octopus."

"Then why did you insist I go out with him?"

"Because I'm afraid you haven't dated since *Gossip Girl*."

Maddie was flummoxed. "You watched *Gossip Girl*?"

"I'm up on current events."

"*Gossip Girl* went off the air years ago."

"Which only illuminates your dating desert."

"Ugh," Maddie groaned. "You're driving me crazy."

"Well, if you're going to accuse me of being the reason you're back in town, I'd better give you a reason," Maude said.

Maddie's face softened. "Granny … ."

"I love you, Maddie girl," Maude said. "I want you to take care of me. I also want to be able to take care of you. What do you need?"

"I don't need anything."

"What about Nick?"

Maddie stiffened. "What about him?"

"What did he do when you found Sadie last night?"

"He wanted to know how I found her."

"What did you tell him?"

"I told him I was sick," Maddie said, her stomach revolting. "I told him it was an accident."

"Did he believe that?"

"Why wouldn't he?"

"Because you're a terrible liar," Maude said. "Also ... he knows you better than anyone, excluding me."

"He doesn't know me anymore."

"Honey, you're the same girl you were ten years ago," Maude said. "You're frozen in time. You haven't been able to move on, and neither has he. You've matured in some ways, but you're still ... his Maddie."

"You know, you were the one who told me that a woman is more than a partner for a man," Maddie pointed out.

"I did," Maude acquiesced. "That doesn't mean that people don't belong together. I certainly belonged to your grandfather. He was the only man who could handle me, and he was the only man I ever loved."

"Were you his property?"

"No," Maude said. "I'm not saying you're Nick's property. I'm saying you're ... his heart."

"He has a girlfriend."

"Who are you trying to convince when you say that?"

"I ... he has a girlfriend."

"He also has a heart," Maude said, refusing to let her granddaughter derail the conversation. "He doesn't love his girlfriend. He does love his heart."

"I don't even know what that means."

"It means that you're his heart," Maude said. "It doesn't matter who his girlfriend is. His girlfriends have always been throwaways. Even he knows that. He's been waiting for you."

Maddie couldn't fight the spilling tears. "What happens when he finds out the truth?"

"What truth?"

"The truth that I'm ... different."

Maude smirked. "He always knew you were different, girl. Most teenage boys run away from girls who are different, and then they run back when they realize that's something to behold.

"Nick never ran," she said. "He never faltered. He never abandoned you. He loved you because you were you. He loved you for ten years after you ran. The truth isn't going to send him screaming for the hills now."

"What are you saying?"

"Give him a chance," Maude said. "I have faith that he will only love you more if you tell him the truth."

"I ... ." Maddie didn't know what to say. Thankfully, the bell ringing over the door of the shop caught her attention. The two giggling teenagers stumbling into the store were more than enough to give her an out – and she took it. "Welcome to Magicks. How can I help you?"

"**ARE** you sure you want to ask that question?"

Maddie hadn't given a tarot card reading since she was a teenager. Still, she knew the basics: Always tell the customer what they wanted to hear. Customers never want bad news. If they get it, they freak out. Jennifer Stilton was asking for just that.

"I need to know," Jennifer said. "If he's going to break up with me, I have to know before I give him my ... peach."

Maddie fought the urge to make a face. "Your ... peach?"

"You know, my Venus Flytrap."

Were teenagers always this stupid? "If you're doubtful about giving him your ... peach ... then don't do it," Maddie said. "That's something you can't take back."

Jennifer studied Maddie seriously. "Who did you give your peach to?"

"I ... ."

"Detective Winters," her friend said, lifting up a candle to study it. "Everyone knows that. They're legendary."

"That's not true," Maddie said, fixing the other girl with a dark look. Jennifer kept referring to her as "Gia." Maddie had no idea what that was short for. "Nick and I are just friends."

"Oh, please," Gia said, rubbing her bottom lip as she returned the candle to the shelf. "Everyone in town knows that you two are soul mates."

"Do you believe in soul mates?" Maddie asked.

"Of course," Gia said. "What else is there to live for?"

Maddie faltered. She hated girls who found their reason for being in men. Of course, she'd done nothing but dwell on Nick for a decade, but that was beside the point. "Yourself."

"Oh, please," Gia scoffed. "There's nothing better than a man in love."

Maddie considered her options. "A man is a great thing," she said, shuffling the tarot cards irritably. "A man isn't everything, though."

"Whatever," Gia said, rolling her eyes. "Don't you have a job to do?"

Maddie tamped down the spurt of anger threatening to erupt from her chest. "Of course." She turned to Jennifer. "Are you sure you want to know if this ... boy ... is going to be your husband?"

"I have to," Jennifer said, waving her hands around haphazardly. "He wants my peach. He says he's going to break up with me if I don't give it to him. I don't want to do it if we're not going to get married."

Maddie was torn ... and disgusted. "You shouldn't base your future decisions on what the cards show," she said. "You should know what you want in your heart." Maddie pressed her eyes shut briefly. *Do you know what you want in your heart?* That inner voice was annoying.

"I want Dustin Bishop," Jennifer said. "I want him to be my ... forever."

Maddie started shuffling the tarot cards resolutely. "Just know, what you see as your forever as a teenager, that's not always your forever as an adult."

"Yeah, great," Gia said. "Shuffle."

Maddie couldn't find anything left to argue about. She flipped up the first card, and then she tried to keep from passing out.

Oh no.

“YOU HAVE TO HELP ME.”

Christy shut one eye, shooting a grotesque wink in Maddie’s direction as she turned the lock on the salon door. “You can’t help the helpless.”

“I’m not helpless,” Maddie said. “I’m … .”

“Stupid?”

“No.”

“Slow?”

“No.”

“Desperate?”

“No. Yes. No. Yes. I … you’re killing me.”

“You need to give me more information, Maddie,” Christy said, nonplussed. “You’ve been a babbling idiot since you came in here twenty minutes ago.”

Maddie was stuck. The tarot cards had shown a little more than Jennifer Stilton’s romantic future. They’d unveiled a murder, and a bloody one at that. Maddie had panicked, regrouped, and then gone for the only bastion of help she could think of. That still didn’t mean she was willing to reveal her true nature. “I … there’s a girl in danger.”

“What girl?”

“Jennifer Stilton.”

“Rebecca Walker’s daughter?”

Maddie was confused. “Rebecca Walker? The girl who was voted prom queen when we were in elementary school?”

“She was also voted Trout Queen at the summer festival.”

“I had no idea Jennifer was her daughter.”

“How did you meet her?” Christy asked.

“She and her friend … I think her name was Gia … came into the store today,” Maddie said. “They wanted readings.”

“Oh, let me guess,” Christy said, arranging the bottles at her station irritably. “Jennifer wanted to know if she would marry Dustin

Bishop. Oh, and Gia – that's short for Virginia, by the way – wanted to make sure he didn't want to marry her."

Maddie was floored. "How did you know that?"

"I know all the teenage girls here," Christy said. "They're chatty little … monsters."

"Monsters?"

"You were an angel when you were a teenager," Christy said. "That's not how most teenagers are. Gia and Jennifer come in here once a month. I know their … drama. They won't shut up."

"Okay," Maddie said carefully. "What's their drama?"

"Dustin Bishop."

"Is he Chad Bishop's kid?"

"Grandkid."

"Ugh. I feel so old."

Christy snickered. "Anyway, he's the new … king."

Maddie knew exactly what Christy was referring to. "He's the boy all the girls want?"

"Yeah," Christy said. "He's the new Todd."

"He's the new Nick," Maddie corrected.

"There aren't many years when you get two kings," Christy said. "This is not one of those years. Dustin is the king. He has the throne unopposed."

"So, all the girls fight about him?"

"He's not much to fight about," Christy said. "In five years, all these girls are going to realize he's a thug in training. They're just too naïve to realize it."

"Is Jennifer the current queen?"

"I guess," Christy said, shrugging. "Dustin has a lot of ladies in waiting, so it's hard to keep the current pecking order straight."

"Well, I need to find Jennifer," Maddie said. "I'm worried she's about to become a cautionary tale."

Christy pursed her lips. "How?"

"I … I can't tell you."

"But it's important, right?"

"It's very important," Maddie said.

Christy sighed. “They’re out at Kissing Point.”

Maddie scowled. “That’s still a thing?”

“All kids need a place to escape to,” Christy said. “Unfortunately, the one here never changes.”

“I need to get out there.”

“Well, let’s go.”

Maddie was stunned. “Wait, you’re going with me?”

“I love drama,” Christy said. “I’m smelling drama. Let’s go.”

Maddie wanted to argue, but she couldn’t muster the energy. “Can you drive?”

14. FOURTEEN

"There are no words."

Christy smirked as she watched Maddie take in the scene. "It's got … personality."

Maddie wasn't naïve. She knew – in the back of her mind, at least – that Kissing Point was where teenagers met to hang out. It had been popular when she was in high school, or that's what her classmates said. Maddie had just never been there before, so she wasn't quite sure what to expect. Six cars parked on top of the bluff – all with steamed up windows – definitely wasn't it.

"Don't they all know everyone else is here?" Maddie asked, glancing at the cars in turn. "And why are the windows steamed up? It's not that cold out."

"You really were the good girl in high school, weren't you?" Christy was enjoying herself. "Okay, let me explain about the birds and bees … ."

"I know about the birds and the bees," Maddie said, scowling.

"Are you sure? You seem to be confused about what these kids are doing."

"I'm not confused." Maddie wrinkled her nose. "I just don't understand why the windows have to be so steamy."

"It's because there's a lot of heavy breathing going on in those cars," Christy said. "There's probably also some petting, and ... yup ... that guy over there hit a home run." Christy pointed toward a four-door sedan that was rocking at the far edge of the bluff.

"Omigod." Maddie slapped her hand over her eyes. "This is so invasive."

"You're the one who wanted to come up here," Christy reminded her.

"I know ... but .... "

"Are you telling me you and Nick never once steamed up a window?" Christy asked. "Not once?"

"How many times do I have to tell you ... ?"

"You were just friends, I know," Christy finished. "Still, there was all that sexual tension between the two of you."

"There was no sexual tension."

"Oh, you're so ... *Little House on the Prairie*."

"What is that supposed to mean?"

"It means you need to be felt up in a car," Christy replied, not backing down. "I'll make sure Nick is aware of your needs."

"Don't you *dare* mention this to him!"

"I still don't know what we're doing here," Christy admitted.

"I needed to find Jennifer."

"Because she's in danger?"

Maddie bit her bottom lip. "Yes."

"And how do you know that?"

"I ... I just do."

"Okay," Christy said, not pressing the issue. "We need to figure out which car is Dustin's."

"You don't know?"

Christy shook her head. "I'm up on the teen gossip. I don't know what they're driving. I barely know what I'm driving."

"Well ... how do we figure out who is in each car?"

Christy shrugged. "There's only one way I know." She stalked up to the first vehicle – a rundown Ford Escort – and banged on the window. "Excuse me."

When no one immediately answered, Christy rolled her eyes and banged again.

"Is it them?" Maddie asked, refusing to move closer to the Escort. She was mortified to be doing this, but she didn't see a way around it.

"I can hear you in there whispering," Christy said, tapping on the window with rampant enthusiasm. "I'm not going to tell your parents. I just need to know who is in here."

Finally, the window lowered. "What do you want?"

"Oh, Hannah Nelson and Aidan Graham," Christy said, studying the occupants for a second. "I didn't know you two were dating."

"Do we get an award?" The voice coming out of the car was male.

"Nope," Christy said. "I'm actually looking for Jennifer Stilton and Dustin Bishop. Are they in one of these cars?"

"Why the hell would I tell you?"

"Well, Aidan, if you don't, I'll tell your mom that you were up here feeling up Hannah when you were supposed to be playing basketball at open gym at the high school," Christy said. "Isn't that what you're supposed to be doing? That's what your mom told me when she was in the salon yesterday."

"I was not feeling her up!"

"Just tell me if Dustin and Jennifer are up here," Christy said. "I'll leave you alone."

"I have no idea," Aidan shot back. "You must be some sick pervert or something if you're up here getting off on watching teenagers make out."

"I thought you weren't doing anything," Christy challenged, hands on hips as she bent down to get a better look inside of the car. "You'd better brush your hair before you go home, Hannah. It's clear you haven't been at the library."

"I ... we were just wrestling."

Maddie snickered.

"Well, it looks like Aidan was winning," Christy said. "So, you really don't know which car is Dustin's?"

"No."

"Fine," Christy said, straightening. "Oh, and Hannah, your shirt is on inside out." Christy rejoined Maddie behind the cars. "I guess we'd better move on to the next one."

"You're going to do that again?" Maddie was flabbergasted.

"Do you have another idea?"

"No."

"Do you want to tell me what's really going on?"

"I ... can't."

"Then we have to do what we have to do," Christy said, moving to the next car to repeat the process. "Open up in the name of the law!"

The window rolled down.

"Oh, David Johnson and Cara Porter," Christy said. "I thought you two broke up."

Maddie tuned the rest of the conversation out. She had no idea how Christy was up on all the teen happenings, but it was fairly amazing. Maddie scanned the four remaining vehicles for a hint, and when a flash of movement at the far end of the bluff caught her attention, she moved toward it.

Even though it was dark, the ambient light from the town filtered up the hill and allowed Maddie to differentiate between the shadows at the tree line. One of the shadows was different. It was human. Kind of.

Maddie sucked in a breath when she realized what she was looking at. "Sarah," she murmured.

"Cara, it's very important that you understand that you don't have to sleep with a boy to keep him interested." Christy was in the middle of a diatribe, and Maddie didn't want to interrupt her, so she started moving toward Sarah on her own. "Twenty seconds of loving from a boy – and I'm being generous – is not worth giving up your self-esteem. If he broke up with you because you wouldn't sleep with him, that means he's a jerk."

Maddie skirted the cars until she was hidden beneath the overhanging boughs of the towering pine trees. She'd lost sight of Sarah, but she had a feeling she was still there. "Sarah?"

"You're the woman who found me in the alley."

Maddie heard the raspy voice before she registered Sarah's filmy countenance again. She'd moved a few feet back, which Maddie was thankful for. "Why are you out here?"

"He's watching."

Maddie stilled, dread washing over her. "Who is watching?"

Sarah tilted her head to the side. "He's looking for someone new."

Maddie was having a hard time following Sarah's train of thought. Could the woman not hear her? Was she still grappling with her new reality? Was she following whoever had hurt her?

Since her interaction with ghosts wasn't limited, Maddie had learned a few tricks over the years. She needed to get Sarah to focus.

"Do you know what happened to you?"

Sarah shifted her gaze from the cars and let it settle on Maddie. The stark sadness reflected on the woman's face was heartbreaking. "I died." She was matter-of-fact.

"Do you know how?"

"I was stabbed."

"Do you remember who did it?" Ghosts are never the same. Some know exactly how they died. Others need time to come to grips with the tragedy, so they refuse to remember. The worst ones are those who can't remember the actual death, and yet they're still bitter anyway. Maddie had no idea what category Sarah would fall into.

"My memory has ... holes."

"That's understandable," Maddie said, her tone calm. "I'm sure it was traumatic."

Sarah barked out a hoarse laugh. "Isn't death always traumatic?"

"If you're not expecting it, yes," Maddie said. "I think some people welcome death."

"That's because they weren't ripped out of a life they weren't done living yet." Sarah was definitely bitter.

Maddie chose her next words carefully. "What can you remember about the time right before you died?"

"Nothing," Sarah said. "I ... it's hard to keep track of things now. It's like I know I'm supposed to be doing something, but I just can't remember what."

Maddie pursed her lips. "Why are you out here tonight?"

Sarah's face pinched as she concentrated. "I can't ... I'm not sure. Why are you out here?"

Maddie saw no sense in lying. "I'm trying to find a teenage girl," she said. "I gave her a tarot card reading this afternoon, and I'm afraid something bad is going to happen to her."

Sarah's face brightened. "Are you a psychic?"

"I ... yes. Kind of." Maddie wasn't sure how to explain the "peculiarity."

"It's too bad I couldn't have met you before I met ... him."

"Who?" Maddie pressed.

"I can't quite remember," Sarah admitted. "I know he's dangerous. I just can't remember who he is."

"You said he was watching."

"He is."

Maddie scanned the cars again. "Is he in one of these cars?"

Sarah shook her head ... confused. "I don't know."

"I have to find Jennifer," Maddie said. "It's really important. She's with a boy named Dustin. Do you know what car they're in?"

"No."

Maddie swallowed her sigh. "Well, I have to find her. Find me at my house. It's the big one on Park Street at the north edge of town. We can talk more then."

Sarah couldn't be Maddie's priority right now, and while she didn't want to abandon the tortured soul, she had more pressing matters to deal with. Maddie swiveled back to the cars, pulling up short when she saw Christy standing a few feet away watching her.

"What are you doing?"

Maddie's cheeks were burning as she tried to come up with a suitable explanation. "I ... ."

Christy arched an eyebrow as she crossed her arms over her chest. "Do you need more time to think of a lie?"

Maddie considered the question. "That would be great. Thanks. Have you checked this car?" She pointed to the nearest one.

"No. I was just about to when I realized you were missing."

"I wasn't missing," Maddie said. "I was just ... exploring."

"The woods?"

"I ... yes. Come on. We have to find Jennifer. She's in trouble."

"Did the trees tell you that?" Christy asked.

Maddie ignored the question and strode up to the car. She squared her shoulders. If Christy could find the courage to interrupt pawing teenagers, there was no reason she couldn't do the same. She rapped on the window. "Open up please."

Christy watched with mild interest.

When nothing happened, Maddie knocked on the window again. "Can you please roll the window down?"

"Go away." A boy had issued the admonishment, but Maddie didn't know if it was the boy she was looking for.

Maddie glanced at Christy, sending a mental plea for help as she considered her options. Christy remained still.

"I just need to know if Jennifer Stilton is in this car," Maddie said.

The teenagers inside whispered for a few seconds. Then the male voice answered. "There's no Jennifer Stilton here. Try the library."

"Oh, okay," Maddie said, biting the inside of her cheek as she considered her options. "Maybe we should check the library?"

"Oh, good grief," Christy said. She stalked to the window of the car and started pounding on it. "Open up right now or I'll call your mothers." Christy scorched Maddie with a look. "You need to get some balls."

"I'm sorry," Maddie muttered. "I've never done this before."

"Do you think I've done this before?"

"You seem like you have."

"Well, I haven't," Christy said. She pounded on the window again. "I will start this car on fire if you don't roll this window down."

Maddie was impressed with Christy's moxie.

"I'm calling the police." The boy in the car was doing all the talking. That made Maddie think they'd found the right couple.

"Go ahead," Christy said. "I think it's a good idea."

Her response must have surprised the boy because Maddie could hear him whispering again. "Listen, you crazy bitch, I'm not joking with you," he said after a moment. "I'm calling the police."

"Good," Christy said. "I'm sure the police would love to talk to your parents about what you're doing up here, Dustin."

The window dropped. Maddie didn't recognize the boy, but Christy clearly did.

"What do you want?"

"I want to talk to Jennifer," Christy said, not missing a beat.

"She's busy."

"Oh, please," Christy scoffed. "I'm sure she'll let you put your hand up her shirt again in a few minutes." Christy hunkered down and stared through the window. "Jennifer, could you come out here, please?"

"What did I do?"

"You didn't do anything," Christy said. "My friend just wants to talk to you."

Maddie watched as Jennifer peered around Christy and focused on her. "You're the woman from the magic shop."

Maddie nodded.

"Why are you here?"

"I … ."

"Just get out of the car," Christy ordered. "I'm really annoyed with this whole thing. I need a stiff drink."

"Then go away," Dustin suggested.

"Don't be obnoxious," Christy warned.

"I've had it," Dustin said. He turned the key in the ignition and the car's engine roared to life. "I'm not listening to one more second of this."

Christy reached into the car and slapped his hand away from the gearshift. "Don't make me hurt you."

"Don't make me hurt *you*," he shot back.

"Just … stop it!"

"You stop it!"

"Get out of that car right now!"

"Get out of my face right now!"

"What is going on?" Jennifer wailed.

The situation was spiraling, and Maddie had no idea how to fix it.

Unfortunately, things got worse when the familiar red and blue associated with a police light started flashing in the night sky.

"Oh, no," Maddie muttered, dropping her face into her hands.

"You're in trouble now, lady!"

"Oh, no, you're in trouble you little … ."

15. FIFTEEN

When Christy started grappling with Dustin over the keys, Maddie thought her night couldn't get any worse. When she saw Nick climb out of the police cruiser and start scanning the assembled Kissing Point visitors – she knew she'd never get over the embarrassment of what was going to come.

"What's going on here?" Nick hadn't seen her yet, Maddie realized. She wondered – briefly – if she had time to flee into the woods.

"There are two crazy women peeking in everyone's windows." The girl from the first car was pointing in their direction.

"I am not crazy, Hannah," Christy snapped. "I'm on a mission of mercy."

Nick shifted his attention to the far side of the bluff, doing a double take when he recognized Maddie. "What the ... ?"

"I want to make a citizen's arrest," Christy announced.

Nick pulled himself together and strode in the direction of Dustin's car. "Why?"

"Because this little ... butthead ... is annoying me."

"You're a butthead," Dustin shot back.

Nick briefly met Maddie's gaze as he moved around her. "Does anyone want to tell me what's going on here?"

"This crazy bitch ... ."

"Choose your words, Dustin," Nick warned.

"This crazy ... old lady ... ."

"Choose different words, Dustin," Christy snapped.

"This crazy ... ."

"Okay, you're cut off," Nick said. He turned to Christy. "Do you want to tell me what's going on here?"

"I just wanted to talk to Jennifer for a second," Christy sniffed.

"Why?"

Christy exchanged a worried look with Maddie. "Um ... ."

Nick shifted his attention to the fidgeting blonde at his side. "Why are you out here?"

"I've never seen it before," Maddie offered lamely. "We were just going for a drive and Christy wanted to show me the bluff."

Nick pursed his lips. "Christy wanted to bring you to Kissing Point?"

"What's wrong with that?"

"I think the better question is: why didn't you ever take her to Kissing Point?" Christy said. "The poor girl had no idea why the windows were so steamy. You've clearly been falling down on the job."

Nick's face flushed. "W-w-what?" He glanced at Maddie. "Did you tell her that?"

"She didn't have to," Christy said. "It's obvious she needs some loving. You should get moving on that."

Nick's heart flopped. He had no idea what Christy was talking about, but part of him was interested in continuing the conversation. One look at Dustin's animated face told him that was a terrible idea – at least for now. "Can someone please explain to me what was going on right before I showed up?"

"I can." Dustin lifted his hand.

"Can you do it without being insulting?"

Dustin nodded.

"Go."

"Jen and I were just sitting up here talking when Ms. Ford started banging on my window."

"Were you talking about if her bra unfastened in the front or the back?" Christy asked.

"Thank you, Christy," Nick snapped. "Go on, Dustin."

"She demanded to talk to Jen," Dustin said. "She was acting weird, and I was afraid she would hurt Jen. When I tried to leave, she tried to take my keys from me – and then she called me a butthead."

"I only called you a butthead after you called me a bitch," Christy countered.

"Why did you two want to talk to Jennifer?" Nick asked. "Jennifer, can you please get out of the car and step around back? Thanks."

Jennifer's long hair was tousled when she finally joined the crowd. Maddie couldn't help but notice that Dustin remained seated in the driver's seat, and she had a sneaking suspicion he was still trying to decide if he could make a hasty escape.

"Were you wrestling, too?" Christy asked as she looked Jennifer up and down.

"Who was wrestling?" Nick asked.

"Hannah and Aidan." Christy pointed to the far end of the bluff. Most of the cars had emptied, and the curious occupants were now watching the spectacle next to Dustin's car. "Aidan was winning."

Nick smirked. "I'm sure he was. So, Jen, can you think of any reason Ms. Ford and Ms. Graves would want to talk to you?"

Jen rubbed her forehead nervously. "Well, I was in Magicks earlier today," she said. "I got a tarot card reading."

Nick faltered, the hair on the back of his neck standing on end. "Really?" His face was unreadable as he looked at Maddie. "What did she tell you about your reading?"

"She told me that sleeping with Dustin to keep him as a boyfriend was a bad idea," Jen admitted, her face twisting. "I had no idea that it would be this bad of an idea."

"Did she tell you anything else?"

"Just that life would be better after high school."

"Uh-huh." Nick ran his tongue over his teeth. Something about this situation – other than the obvious – was irritating him. "Do you have anything you want to add to this conversation, Ms. Graves?"

"I was just worried about her," Maddie said, her voice barely a whisper. "I didn't want her to get hurt."

"I wouldn't hurt her," Dustin said.

"You've got 'tool' written all over you," Christy said.

"You're mean," Dustin grumbled.

"That doesn't mean I'm wrong."

Nick pinched the bridge of his nose. "Okay, here's what's going to happen," he said. "Dustin, you're going to take Jen home, and I mean immediately home. I'm going to be checking in exactly ten minutes, and if she's not there, you're going to jail."

"But … ."

Nick wagged his finger in Dustin's face to cut off the argument. "Don't make me arrest you now." He turned to Jen. "Ms. Graves is right, you do not want to sleep with him. You'll regret it for the rest of your life."

"You all suck," Dustin muttered.

Nick glanced at Christy. "You need to stop harassing teenagers at Kissing Point," he said before shifting his attention to Maddie. "And you need to … ."

"Get kissed?" Christy suggested.

Nick swallowed hard. "Can I trust you to get Maddie back home without another detour?"

Christy snapped her feet together and saluted. "Yes, sir."

Nick fought the mad urge to laugh. This whole evening was … surreal. "Just … go home. I don't want to see you two up here again. You're too old."

"Oh, shut it," Christy said. She grabbed Maddie's arm and started dragging her across the bluff. "This night just blows."

Once they got back to Christy's car, Maddie fixed Christy with an apologetic look. "I'm so sorry."

"Oh, it's fine," Christy said, waving off Maddie's words.

The two women watched Nick climb back into his work cruiser and drive away. Once he was gone, Christy focused on Maddie intently.

"So, do you want to tell me how long you've been psychic?"

. . .

MADDIE WAS positive her throat was closing up. There could be no other explanation for the huge ball that was lodged in her windpipe and preventing oxygen from making its way to her lungs.

"Do you need a moment?" Christy asked, leaning her back against her car as she watched Maddie worriedly. "You're not going to pass out, are you?"

Maddie shook her head, but the effort was enough to knock her off balance. She sank to the ground to keep herself from tumbling headfirst into it.

Christy plopped down next to her and ran a soothing hand over her back. "Don't freak out," she said. "I kind of had suspicions in high school. Tonight just sealed the deal for me."

Maddie finally found her voice. "How did you know?"

"You were a quiet kid, Maddie," Christy said. "You weren't invisible, though. I saw you in the cemetery one day. It was right after Mark Garvey died when I first figured it out. You were standing in front of his grave."

Maddie's face colored. "How do you know I wasn't talking to myself?"

"I considered it," Christy said. "Your mother ran a magic shop, though. It made more sense that you were psychic."

"But … ."

Christy cut her off. "There's nothing wrong with it. It doesn't scare me. I don't think you're a bad person."

"I'm a freak," Maddie muttered. No one outside of her own family – except Kincaid – had ever known her secret.

"You're not a freak," Christy said. "You're just different. I don't see why you're making such a big deal about this. I think it's really cool. I'm totally taking you to the casino over in Traverse City."

Christy's jocularity jolted Maddie out of self-pity mode. "That's not really how it works."

"So, how does it work?"

"I … sometimes I just know things," Maddie said. "Sometimes I know things because of dreams, and sometimes I see them when I'm awake."

"Is that how you found the body?"

"No. That was an accident. That's how I saw the body's ghost, though. That's how I knew her name before the police released it."

"The police still haven't released it," Christy said. "Who was it?"

"Her name was Sarah Alden."

Christy searched her memory. "That doesn't sound familiar to me. Was she from here?"

Maddie shrugged. "I haven't had a chance to talk to her yet," she said. "Tonight was the first time, and I was more interested in finding Jennifer than talking to her. She says she has holes in her memory. It will take some time for those to firm up."

"Wow," Christy said. "How many ghosts have you talked to?"

"I don't know."

"Give me an estimate."

"A hundred."

"That is so cool," Christy said, her mind working. "We should totally hold a séance. Do you think we could talk to a celebrity ghost?"

"No," Maddie said. She grabbed Christy's arm and squeezed it tightly. "You can't tell anyone. If people know … ."

"Don't worry, Maddie," Christy said, jerking her arm away and rubbing it ruefully. "Your secret is safe with me. I haven't told anyone before now."

"You didn't know until now."

"I knew," Christy said. "I just kept it to myself."

Maddie sighed, forcing herself to relax. "Thank you."

"It's going to be okay, Maddie," Christy said. "I promise. You're overreacting."

"My mom always told me it had to remain a secret."

"I understand," Christy said. "Blackstone Bay is a small town. I don't think the people would react as poorly as you seem to think they would, though. What does Nick think?"

Maddie stilled.

"Oh, you haven't told him?" Christy was beside herself. "How did you hide it?"

"I just never told him," Maddie said. "I didn't want to lose him."

"And you think that telling him the truth would make you lose him?"

"Of course," Maddie said, her voice rising. "If he knew … ."

"He would just love you more," Christy said.

"You can't be serious."

"I'm deadly serious," Christy said. "You built a wall between the two of you because you were scared to tell him the truth. If you tear down that wall, there will be nothing standing between you. Don't you want that?"

More than anything, Maddie thought. "He'll never look at me the same way again."

"Probably not," Christy agreed. "That doesn't mean he won't look at you in a better way. It's your secret, though. You can tell him when you're ready."

"I'll never be ready."

"Never say never, Maddie Graves," Christy said, laughing as she got to her feet and brushed off the seat of her pants. She extended her hand and helped Maddie to a standing position. "I happen to be a little psychic myself, and I can clearly see that you and Nick are on a crash course toward one another. How you handle it is up to you."

16. SIXTEEN

By the next afternoon, Maddie had almost managed to convince herself that Christy would keep her secret. She had no doubt the effervescent redhead had every intention of keeping things to herself, but Christy was gossipy by nature. There was no way Maddie could be sure. She just had to have faith.

When the bell over the door at Magicks jangled, Maddie almost expected Christy to be standing there with half the town – some of them with pitchforks and torches – so Todd's arrival threw her for an obvious loop.

"Hello," Todd said, smiling brightly.

"Hi." Maddie felt like a deer caught in headlights. He'd called her three different times since their disastrous date, and Maddie had conveniently dodged each call. She had no idea why he was here now. He couldn't possibly want a repeat of that torturous experience.

"You've been a little hard to reach," Todd said, wandering around the store so he could take in the ambiance and kitschy trinkets. "I figured, if I wanted to talk to you, it would have to be face to face."

"I … I've been really busy."

"I heard," Todd said. "Are you spending all of your nights up at Kissing Point with Christy Ford these days? Is that why you're dodging my calls?"

Maddie's face colored. "We were just out for a drive."

"At Kissing Point?"

"I'd never been there before." Maddie felt like an idiot.

"That's because you spent all of your time with Nick Winters in high school," Todd said. "He has no idea how to please a woman."

Maddie balked. "I really wish you wouldn't talk about Nick like that."

"Why?"

"Because he's my friend," Maddie said. "I don't like it when people talk badly about my friends."

"And he's just your friend, right?"

"I've already answered that question."

"You have," Todd agreed. "That was before he interrupted our date and tried to dump his girlfriend on me so he could take you home, though."

Maddie had no idea how to respond to that. "Is that why you're here?"

"I'm here for you," Todd said. "I thought we should try dating again."

"You can't be serious."

"Oh, I'm serious," Todd said. "I feel I was at a disadvantage at the restaurant. After Winters' little show, it was impossible for me to measure up. I'd like a chance to wow you on my own terms."

"And how are you going to wow me?"

"When is your lunch break?" Todd asked.

Maddie glanced at the clock on the wall. "Fifteen minutes."

Todd sat down in one of the open wingback chairs next to the front window and plastered a bright smile on his face. "Wow. What great timing."

"For what?"

"I'll show you in fifteen minutes."

"But … ."

"Finish your work," Todd said. "I don't want any distractions. I have a surprise for you."

Maddie sucked in her cheeks. She didn't like the look on his face.

It was almost … animalistic. She was legitimately worried the surprise he wanted to show her was in his pants. "I … ."

"You can't say no," Todd said. "I deserve a second chance after the first one blew up in my face because of your … friend."

Maddie sighed. "Fine. Fifteen minutes."

"WHEN YOU SAID you had a surprise, I didn't realize it was on my front lawn." Maddie studied the blanket and picnic basket Todd had laid out under the large elm dubiously. "Are you really taking me on a picnic?"

"I was under the impression that you liked picnics," Todd said, settling on the blanket and patting the spot next to him. "Didn't you and Winters spend your teenage years having picnics in the woods?"

Maddie frowned. Todd was obsessed with Nick. Part of her understood it. He was trying to ascertain if Nick was competition. The problem was Todd always looked at Nick as competition – no matter what they were competing for. Maddie had trouble believing she was anything more than just another trophy for his shelf, something to lord over Nick.

Of course, that wasn't the only problem. Despite how handsome he was, Maddie wasn't even remotely attracted to Todd. She had to find a way to let him down without making it seem like she was calling his manhood into question. That would only make him redouble his efforts. She was sure of that. "Your obsession with Nick worries me," Maddie admitted.

"Excuse me? I am not obsessed with Winters."

"You bring him up constantly."

"Maybe that's because he's always in my face."

Maddie sighed. Arguing the point wasn't going to make her case. She needed time to think of another plan. "What's in the basket?"

Todd shot her a lazy smile. "Open it."

Maddie indulged him. "Is this chicken salad?"

"It is. You like chicken salad, don't you?"

"It's good," Maddie said. "Is this from Ruby's?"

"I only buy the best for my dates."

Maddie couldn't figure out how Todd equated smugness with charm, but he clearly did. "Well, let's eat," Maddie said. "I only have an hour before I have to open the store again, and I'm sure you have to get back to the dealership."

"I'm the boss," Todd countered. "I employ people to make sure the dealership runs smoothly."

"Oh, I'm sure you're invaluable to the operation," Maddie said, feeding his ego. "You can't become the boss if you're not, can you?"

"You're a smart woman," Todd said. "When you add your intelligence to your smoking-hot body, you're the perfect package."

After mentally rolling her eyes so hard she almost tipped over, Maddie forced a tight smile onto her face. "So, tell me, how is it that you're not married yet?" An idea was starting to form, and she wanted to test the boundaries of it.

"I'm not really ready for marriage," Todd said, digging into his sandwich enthusiastically. "I like to practice for it, though."

His wink was so disgusting Maddie momentarily wondered if she would be capable of hiding his body if she choked him with the sandwich he was inhaling. After giving up on the idea – Maude wasn't strong enough to help her drag Todd through the woods without anyone noticing, and the wheelbarrow was broken – Maddie continued with the next step of her plan. "But you must want children," she said.

"Not really."

"Oh, come on," Maddie said. "I want at least five of them."

Todd coughed, clearing his throat. "Five?"

"Yeah," Maddie said brightly. "I'm going to have to get going soon. I'm going to be thirty in two years."

"So, you're saying … ."

"My biological clock is ticking away," Maddie said. "Tick. Tick. Tick." She rubbed his hand suggestively. "I'll bet a car dealership could easily support five kids."

"I … are you being serious?"

"Of course," Maddie said. "I've always dreamed of a big family."

"And what about Winters?" Todd asked. "Does he want a big family, too?"

"You'll have to ask him," Maddie said. "We never really talked about it. I don't see how it matters. It's not like I plan on having kids with him." It was a calculated risk.

"Are you just saying that to placate me?"

"Nope. It's the truth."

Todd narrowed his eyes. "Do you really want five children?"

"Absolutely," Maddie said. "This sandwich is great, by the way. We should plan another dinner."

Todd balked. "I'm not sure ... I'm really busy this week."

"Oh, come on," Maddie said. "I thought you wanted a real date?"

"I do," Todd replied hurriedly. "I just think ... I'll look at my calendar and get back to you."

Maddie smirked. "That sounds great." Mission accomplished.

"**SO,** WHAT DID THAT JACKASS WANT?"

Maude was sitting in one of the chairs and staring out the window when Maddie returned to the store.

"Oh, he wanted to mark his territory," Maddie said. "He wants to make sure word gets around that we're dating."

Maude snorted. "He wants to make sure that word gets around to Nick that you're dating."

"Yeah, I got that feeling, too," Maddie said. "I don't think he's interested in me. He's just interested in getting a dig in at Nick."

"I've always hated Todd Winthrop," Maude said. "He always thought he was such a ... lothario."

"Lothario?"

"You know, a ladies' man."

"He still thinks that," Maddie said.

"So, why did you agree to have a picnic with him?"

"Because he wouldn't leave."

"He's such a douche."

"Granny," Maddie scolded. "You shouldn't say things like that."

"Am I wrong?"

"No."

"Are you going to go out with him again?" Maude asked.

"Why? Do you think I should?"

Maude bit her lip, considering. "Maybe."

"You just said … ."

"Yes, but the more you go out with Todd, the more Nick will freak out," Maude explained. "Nick will break a lot quicker if Todd is in the picture."

Maddie faltered. "What are you talking about?"

"You know exactly what I'm talking about," Maude said. "This little-girl thing you're running doesn't work on me."

"I have no idea what you're talking about," Maddie said stubbornly.

"You know exactly what I'm talking about," Maude said. "You want Nick to be jealous. Admit it."

Maddie pressed her lips together and mulled the statement over. *Was that true?* "I don't want Nick to be jealous," Maddie said finally. "I want Nick to be … happy."

"No, you want Nick to be happy with you," Maude corrected. "Let's stop playing games here. You didn't just come home for me."

"Granny, I love you."

"I love you, too, Maddie girl," Maude said. "You still came home for Nick."

"Nick has a girlfriend."

"Oh, you're like a broken record. Do you want to know what I think?"

"Not really."

Maude ignored her. "I think you're relieved Nick has a girlfriend right now. You know he doesn't have real feelings for her, so you're safe trying to figure things out without losing him."

"That is just … ridiculous."

"I'm right," Maude said. "I'm always right, by the way, but I'm especially right on this front. You're trying to come to grips with your 'peculiarity,' and that means you're eventually going to have to tell

Nick. When you do, and he doesn't shun you, you're going to have to accept that he's your match."

"I ... Christy knows."

Maude raised her eyebrows, surprised. "You told her? I'm proud of you."

"I didn't tell her." Maddie told Maude about the previous night's excursion.

"Wow, that's a lot of information for one old woman to absorb," Maude said. "Okay, first off, how much danger do you think the Stilton girl is in?"

"I don't think it's good."

"Well, we need to keep an eye on her," Maude said. "I think most of the teenagers in this town are dead weight, but she's one of the good ones."

"I would be worried about her if she was one of the bad ones, too."

"That's because you're a walking angel," Maude said. "I'm going to ignore the Nick situation. I have a feeling he's piecing things together on his own. He'll approach you when he's ready."

Maddie was floored. "No. He can't ... ."

"The boy isn't dumb," Maude said. "He's been searching for a reason for years. He wants to know why you cut ties. He needs a reason before he can woo you. Now that you're back in town, it won't take him long to find that reason because he desperately wants to woo you. This is good."

"This is not good," Maddie argued. "And who says woo anymore?"

"You're right," Maude said, patting her hand. "This is not good. It's actually great. What about Christy? Do you think she'll tell anyone?"

"She says she won't."

"Then she won't."

"But ... she's gossipy."

"She's also loyal," Maude pointed out. "She won't betray you."

"I hope you're right," Maddie said, rubbing her forehead. "I just wish ... I just wish I could be sure."

Maude wrinkled her nose. "Have you talked to your mother about this yet?"

For the second time in less than five minutes, her grandmother had managed to stun Maddie. "You know she's here?"

"I know," Maude said. "She won't leave until I do."

"Why do you think that?"

"Because a mother is never supposed to outlive her child," Maude said, fighting back tears. "How is she?"

"She's good," Maddie said. "I think she's still trying to get a hold of the whole … ."

"Death?"

Maddie nodded. "She shows up out of the blue, and then she disappears for a couple of days."

"Well, she'll get used to it," Maude said. "The next time she's here … can you… ?" Maude looked uncertain.

Maddie reached over and clasped her grandmother's hand warmly. "We'll all have tea."

"I'm going to have bourbon in mine," Maude said, pushing the serious thoughts out of her mind.

"Well, that sounds fun."

Maude shook her head to dislodge the melancholy. "So, let's go back to talking about Nick. How long do you think it will be until you two hit the sheets?"

Maddie pressed her eyes shut. It was like an ongoing nightmare, and she just couldn't wake up.

17. SEVENTEEN

When Sarah Alden found her again, Maddie was ready. It had been almost twenty-four hours since the woman had disappeared on the bluff. Maddie had no idea if she'd remained to watch the show, but when Sarah appeared on the front porch of Magicks the next night, Maddie was sitting outside and sipping from a glass of iced tea.

"I knew you'd find me."

"How did you know?" Sarah's form was more solid. She'd obviously been practicing.

"Because you want to be able to rest," Maddie said.

"Is that what all ghosts want?"

"I think so," Maddie said. "I think there are some who want to stay for other reasons." Her mind traveled to Olivia momentarily. She hadn't been lying when she told Maude she hadn't seen her mother in days. She was starting to get worried. "I think most people just want to make sure that everything is going to be okay with their loved ones so they can move on."

"That's not what I want."

"What do you want?"

"Retribution."

Maddie nodded, understanding. “You want to make sure that whoever killed you pays, don’t you?”

“Is that wrong?”

“No,” Maddie said. “I want to help you.”

“Because you want him to pay?”

“Because I want you to be able to rest,” Maddie replied. “And also because I don’t want anyone else to get hurt.”

“So, how do we start?” Sarah asked.

“Well, I need information,” Maddie said. “The police haven’t made your name public yet. I’m not sure if that’s normal for Blackstone Bay. It’s not normal for the city. Most homicide victims are known within twenty-four hours in Detroit, for example. When I mentioned your name to my friend, she didn’t recognize it. Did you live in Blackstone Bay?”

“Is that where I am?”

“Yes.”

“I’ve been here before,” Sarah said, her movements across the front porch mimicking pacing (even though she had no feet). “I want to say I haven’t been here for years, but I’m not sure that’s true.”

“What do you remember about your life?”

“I was a secretary for a law office in Traverse City.”

“Is that where you lived?”

Sarah shook her head. “I actually lived in Williamsburg. It’s a really small town just outside of Traverse City.”

“Okay. That’s a start. Were you dating anyone?”

Sarah sighed. “I think so.”

“That’s fuzzy, too?”

“Yes.”

“Well, I can’t be sure, but I think that you’re fighting your memories,” Maddie said.

“You’ve dealt with this before?”

“Unfortunately.”

“So, how do you cure it?”

“Most spirits eventually just remember,” Maddie said. “As they get stronger, they get more control.”

"You don't want to wait for that to happen, do you?"

Maddie shook her head. "I have a bad feeling."

"About the girl in the car last night?"

"I have a bad feeling about her, too," Maddie admitted. "I'm just not sure if the bad feelings are related."

"Can't you ask your ... spirit friends?"

Maddie smirked. "I don't have spirit friends. Well, I do, but my 'peculiarity' doesn't work like that."

"How does it work?"

"If I knew, I'd find a way to shut it off."

"Why? You're helping people."

"Am I?"

"You're helping me," Sarah said. "I have a feeling I'm not the first ghost you've tried to help."

"I don't always succeed."

"No one does," Sarah said. "Why should you be any different?"

Maddie shrugged. She had no answer to the question. "I think we need to try and jog your memory."

"You want to go back to the alley, don't you?"

Maddie nodded.

"Let's go."

"Are you sure? It might be traumatic."

"More traumatic than dying?"

"Probably not," Maddie conceded. "You don't really remember dying, though."

"Oh, that's where you're wrong," Sarah said. "I don't remember much else, but I remember dying clearly. I remember gasping for breath. I remember the blood pooling in my lungs and drowning me from the inside. I remember a man standing over me and watching me until the last breath left my body."

"That's horrible."

"I remember dying," Sarah said. "I need to remember who did it."

"Okay," Maddie said, getting to her feet. "Let's take a walk."

. . .

"IT LOOKS DIFFERENT IN THE DARK," Sarah complained.

Maddie had been careful during the walk, making sure no one was lurking in the shadows and listening to her talk to herself. Once she got to the alley, she was reasonably sure no one would discover her. One rule of a small town is that it basically shuts down after dark. Even the twenty-four-hour minimart on the edge of town closed before midnight. It was still relatively early, especially by city standards, but the streets of Blackstone Bay were empty.

"Okay, go back to when you died," Maddie instructed. "Was it light or dark?"

"Dark," Sarah said.

"Put yourself back in your body," Maddie said.

"Oh, I wish," Sarah grumbled.

"You know what I mean," Maddie said, ignoring the sarcasm. "You were on the ground here." Maddie pointed. "Can you, I don't know, lay down?"

"I don't have a body."

"You can pretend."

Sarah scowled, but she did as she was told. Maddie didn't take the attitude personally. She knew Sarah wasn't really mad at her. She was just mad at the situation.

"Okay," Maddie said. "You're looking up. Where was he standing?" Sarah pointed and Maddie moved to the spot. "Here?"

"Yes."

"How tall was he?"

"About six inches taller than you."

Maddie did the math in her head. "That puts him right around six feet. What does his body look like?"

"He's fit. He's got broad shoulders. His waist is narrow. He clearly works out."

"What is he wearing?"

"It's hard to tell," Sarah said. "Everything he's wearing is dark. His coat is longer, though."

"Like a trench coat?"

"Yes."

"Okay. Good. What about his hair?"

"It's too dark to see a color."

"Is it longer or shorter?"

"It's medium length, kind of brushy on top," Sarah said.

"Good. Does he say anything?"

"No."

Maddie was disappointed.

"Wait. He whispers something."

"What?"

"Was it good for you."

"That's what he wants to know?" Maddie was horrified.

Sarah nodded.

Maddie swallowed. "Think hard. Do you recognize his voice?"

"It's familiar," Sarah said. "I just can't place where."

"That's good," Maddie said, trying to encourage Sarah. "It's a good start."

"We still don't know who it is."

"We know more, though," Maddie said.

Sarah was back on her feet. Her transparent body had gone rigid, and she was peering into the darkness behind Maddie. "Someone is coming."

Maddie's blood ran cold. She turned quickly, ready to defend herself. The figure that appeared in the dim moonlight was a familiar one, and it filled Maddie with dread.

"What are you doing here, Mad?"

NICK HAD no idea what made him turn down the alley when he left the police station on his way home. His mind had been busy all day, his interaction with Maddie and Christy the previous evening plaguing him. He knew he was close to figuring out Maddie's secret. He was just missing one piece.

The alley wasn't technically on his way home, but he wanted to check it out again in the dark. The scene had been officially cleared the day before. The state crime team claimed there was nothing of interest left there to discover. Nick wasn't so sure.

When he started down the alley, he was lost in thought. He didn't expect to discover anything. He really just wanted to take a look. The case wasn't even technically his, but it's not every day that murder visits Blackstone Bay. It was cause for concern for everyone, including him.

When he heard a voice, he slowed his pace. He was hopeful that he was about to discover something. As he got closer, he realized he recognized the voice, and the bottom dropped out of his world.

"What are you doing here, Mad?"

Maddie's body was rigid, but her face softened when he moved closer. "Nicky?"

"Yeah, it's me."

"What are you doing here?" Maddie asked, confused.

"I think I'm the one asking questions right now," Nick said, his tone grim. "I asked you first."

"I … I was just taking a walk."

Nick didn't believe her for a second. Maddie had never overtly lied to him – at least as far as he knew – but she was lying now. She was on edge. "You were taking a walk in the alley where you discovered a body?"

"I … ."

"Don't lie to me again, Maddie," Nick ordered. "Don't you dare lie to me."

"Nicky … ."

"Tell me what you're doing here."

Maddie's eyes filled with tears. Nick could see them – still unshed, but not for long – glinting in the corners of her eyes. "If I tell you, you'll never talk to me again."

Nick didn't care. "Tell me."

"Please, Nicky," Maddie said, her voice breaking. "I don't … you'll hate me."

"I don't think that's possible," Nick said. "I need to know, though. I deserve to know. You owe me. What are you doing here?"

Maddie sucked in a breath, her chest heaving. "I'm psychic. I can also talk to ghosts. I was here talking to Sarah Alden, trying to get her to remember who killed her."

Nick pressed his eyes shut. The information should have surprised him, but it didn't. He'd caught himself wondering that very thing since his conversation with Detective Kincaid earlier in the week. Then, when Maddie discovered a terrified and frightened child, his suspicions had kicked into overdrive. After that, he'd spent days wracking his childhood memories for clues. When he looked back – when he studied those years with Maddie through the eyes of an adult – he saw a lot of things he'd missed. "How long have you known?"

Maddie shifted uncomfortably. "Since elementary school."

Nick nodded stiffly. "Did Olivia know?"

"Yes."

"Was she ... like you?"

"Yes."

"What about Maude?"

"No."

"She knows, though, doesn't she?"

"She does."

Nick pressed his lips together and inhaled deeply through his nose. He ran his hand through his hair as he considered how to progress. "What did Sarah Alden tell you?"

"I ... you don't want to ask more questions about me?"

"I do," Nick said. "I need to collect myself. I need to focus on something else right now, so we're going to talk about Sarah Alden while I think."

"Okay," Maddie said, fighting to keep her voice even as she recounted her session with Sarah. When she was done, she watched Nick expectantly.

"That's not much to go on, but I'll see if any of it can help," Nick said. "Tell me about Jennifer. Why were you really at Kissing Point last night?"

"I saw danger in her cards."

"What kind of danger?"

"It was nothing specific," Maddie said. "That's why I had to find her."

"Is she in danger from the man who killed Sarah?"

"I don't know."

"Could the danger you felt revolve around Dustin?" Nick asked.

"I don't know."

"What do you know?" Nick snapped.

Maddie reared back in the face of his anger. "The visions don't come with a road map."

Nick held up his hands to still her. "I'm sorry I yelled. I didn't mean to scare you. I'm just ... I'm really pissed at you."

"Because I'm a freak," Maddie said, her voice small. "I told Maude this would happen."

"Maude wanted you to tell me, didn't she?"

"Yes."

"What about Olivia?"

Maddie gripped the ends of her long hair with both hands worriedly. "Mom always told me never to tell anyone. She said ... she said people wouldn't understand. She said people would ostracize me if they knew."

"Even me?"

"She never talked about you specifically."

Nick licked his lips, his mind busy as he tried process everything. "I need to think about this."

"I know."

"I'm just so ... you lied to me," Nick said, his heart twisting painfully. "You lied to me for our whole lives."

"I was scared to tell you."

"Why? Did you think I would tell someone?"

"No," Maddie said. "I thought you would run away, and you were the best friend I ever had. I was terrified of losing you."

"So, you shut me out and forged a new life because you were scared to tell me," Nick said. "That's what happened, isn't it?"

"I ... yes."

"Was it worth it, Maddie?" Nick hissed, taking a step away from her. He was so angry he was afraid he would shake her if he didn't put some distance between them. "Was it worth shredding everything to keep a secret that didn't need to be kept?"

"I … ."

Nick couldn't listen to one more lame excuse. "Just don't."

"Nicky … ."

Nick raised his hand to ward off whatever she was about to say. "I can't even look at you right now."

"Nicky … ." Maddie's voice was anguished.

"Go home, Maddie," Nick said. "Just … go home. I need to think."

18. EIGHTEEN

Nick stared out at the stars from his back porch, lost in thought as he warded off the cold. He should've been in bed hours ago – an early morning shift at the police department was looming – but his mind was clouded.

Why hadn't she just told him? Why was she so terrified of what he would do? Was he so bad of a friend that he'd given her a reason to believe he would walk away?

Maddie had always been shy. When they'd met on the first day of kindergarten, Maddie spent the morning cowering in the corner while the rest of the kids played – and mercilessly teased her. Nick had been drawn to her – even then – and the overwhelming urge to protect her manifested early.

By the time they hit middle school, that protective instinct was ingrained in his very being. If anyone even looked at her funny, he would pound them. When high school hit, Nick's chest was broad enough to absorb the vitriol lobbed at her from every direction. He always recognized what it was: jealousy. Maddie was sweet, and she was beautiful, and she was thoughtful. That scared the girls who didn't measure up.

How could she possibly think he would ever just abandon her?

Nick had seen the fear on her face right before she told him. She was resigned. She fully expected him to shun her. Was that what he wanted? "Dammit, Maddie," he mumbled, rubbing the crease between his eyebrows.

Nick wasn't really angry at her. Part of him understood the fear. She was different. He'd always known that. The oddities of her personality were what kept him close. She could make him laugh faster – and harder – than anyone else in the world. She could make him feel comfort with a simple touch when he was upset. She was his ... everything.

He still felt betrayed.

Nick wasn't having trouble rationalizing her fear. He was having trouble understanding her doubt.

As Nick studied the stars, one of them turned nuclear and shot across the sky. "Make a wish," he whispered. He clamped his eyes shut as his most fervent – and frequent – wish flitted through his mind. When he opened his eyes, he saw a slight figure hovering at the far end of the patio. "Maddie?"

The figure shifted. "No."

Crap. "Cassidy? What are you doing here?"

Cassidy moved around the railing and climbed the steps of the porch. "I was taking a chance you were up."

"It's after midnight," Nick said. "You shouldn't be out this late. It's not safe."

"Well, I was driving to a police detective's house, so I figured I was perfectly fine," Cassidy teased.

She was dressed in a long coat, and Nick's stomach twisted at the sight of it. He had a feeling he knew what was underneath, and it was nothing he wanted to see. Cassidy was becoming more and more desperate with her attempts to entice him, and each move made Nick more and more determined to find a way to break up with her. He was just ... done.

"I'm really tired, Cassidy," Nick said. "I think you should go home. I need some sleep."

Cassidy's face fell momentarily, but the set of her jaw became determined as she straightened. "I'm here to help you sleep."

"I don't think you are."

Cassidy's hands moved to the front of her coat, and she threw it open dramatically. She was completely nude underneath. Nick had no idea if she thought the show was supposed to be hot, but the revelation left Nick cold. "I'm not really in the mood."

Cassidy faltered. "What?"

"Listen, it's nice that you went out of your way to come and see me," Nick said, grasping for a way to let her save some modicum of self-respect. "I'm just ... I'm really tired."

"Too tired for this?" Cassidy gestured to her naked body. She was fit, her breasts large and firm, and most men would've jumped her the second they saw her. Nick wasn't most men.

"I'm tired, Cassidy."

Cassidy licked her lips and shifted her head so she wasn't facing Nick. "We haven't spent any time together in a week."

"We went to dinner," Nick replied.

"And you picked a fight with Todd Winthrop and offered to let him take me home so you could take ... someone else ... home with you."

"That was just an old rivalry," Nick said, rubbing the back of his neck. "I also took you to the fair."

"And then you left me there ... alone ... while you chased *someone else* and disappeared for an hour."

"I found a missing child," Nick pointed out.

"You did," Cassidy agreed, closing her coat and wrapping her arms around her waist. "You didn't leave to find a child, though. You left to take care of Maddie."

"She was sick."

"Nick, I don't ... ever since Maddie returned to Blackstone Bay, you've been distant."

"I think you're exaggerating."

"Really? We haven't had sex in almost two weeks. It's not like you're an animal, but you usually don't turn me down."

"I'm not turning you down," Nick said. "I'm just ... tired."

"Because of Maddie?"

Nick couldn't go down that slippery slope. "Because there was a murder in town. We all have a lot of work to do."

"So, you're denying your sudden disinterest in me has something to do with Maddie?"

"Maddie and I are just friends."

"Right," Cassidy said, unconvinced. "That's why, when you look at her, you look like you want to crawl into her skin and live there with her. Just the two of you."

Nick knew he shouldn't be annoyed. He knew he was the one wronging her. The accusation grated on him, though. "You don't know anything about me."

"I know that we were happy until Maddie came back to town."

She was obviously oblivious. "My life doesn't revolve around Maddie," Nick said. "It also doesn't revolve around you. I have a job to do. A woman died. Get some perspective, Cassidy."

Cassidy's face contorted.

"I'm sorry if I'm hurting your feelings, I really am, but I didn't invite you here," Nick said. "I need some sleep, and you need to go home. Stop worrying about Maddie, and start worrying about yourself. That would be a great way to start a new day."

With those words, Nick left Cassidy standing in the back yard and disappeared into his house, locking the door behind him for good measure. He felt guilty for being so harsh with her, but he was so twisted by Maddie's admission earlier in the night he couldn't focus on anything else.

He had decisions to make, and he couldn't make them without some sleep. Everything would be better in the morning. He was almost sure of it.

"YOU LOOK like you've been run over by a truck."

Maddie jerked when Olivia popped into view. She was curled up in the window seat in the front of the store, her eyes red and puffy from hours of crying, and she'd fully expected to pass out from sheer exhaustion around dawn. Olivia had created the window seat – which was larger than normal – just so Maddie could read in the store when she was a child. It was the place she retreated to when she was upset.

"Where have you been?"

"Nowhere," Olivia replied truthfully. "Why? How long have I been gone?"

"Days."

Olivia moved toward her daughter, studying her face with a worried expression. "What happened?"

"Nick knows."

"Nick knows what?"

"He *knows*!"

"Oh," Olivia said, lowering her voice thoughtfully. "You finally told him?"

"He caught me at a crime scene talking to a ghost."

"That's ... unfortunate," Olivia said. "How did he take it?"

"How do you think he took it?" Maddie was beyond rational thought.

"I think he was probably angry," Olivia said, moving to the window seat and hovering as close to her daughter as she could manage. "I wish I could hug you right now."

Maddie ignored the sentiment. "He was furious."

"Did he yell at you?"

"He said he couldn't even look at me."

Olivia sighed. "He didn't mean it, Maddie."

"He meant it," Maddie said, burying her face in one of the pillows so she could hide her misery. "He hates me. I knew this would happen. Maude said he would accept it. Christy said he would accept it. I knew, though. I knew he would hate me."

"Oh, Maddie, stop being so dramatic," Olivia chided. "You're not a teenager anymore."

Maddie was stunned. "Excuse me?"

"Nick could never hate you," Olivia said. "He's loved you for as long as I've known him. He's loved you for as long as he's known you. He just feels betrayed."

"He thinks I'm a freak," Maddie countered.

"He thinks no such thing," Olivia scoffed. "He's not angry because of what you are, sunshine. He's angry because he feels like he's been lied to. He doesn't understand why you kept it secret."

"I told him it was all your fault," Maddie admitted. "I told him you told me to keep it a secret."

"I never told you to keep it a secret from him," Olivia countered. "I told you to keep it secret until you could trust someone. There is a difference."

"But … ."

"No, don't you dare blame this on me," Olivia said. "I never understood why you didn't tell him. If anyone could accept it – if anyone could understand – Nick is the person."

"But you told me that people would be scared of me if I told them," Maddie protested.

"I told you to be careful with your secret," Olivia said. "I never once doubted that Nick would accept you and still love you."

Maddie moaned into the pillow. "Now you tell me."

Olivia mimed brushing her hand over Maddie's hair. She couldn't give her daughter the comfort she so desperately needed, but she could give her a good, hard dose of reality. "Nothing is ruined here, Maddie."

"Nick said he couldn't even look at me!"

"He's hurt because you lied, not because you're different," Olivia said. "He's also the most forgiving boy – man, he's a man now – that I've ever met. Things will be okay."

"He hates me."

"You're being ridiculous," Olivia said. "Nick could never hate you."

"Well, he does."

"Maddie, Nick Winters is the most loyal individual I've ever seen," Olivia said. "He's always loved you. He will always love you. It's in his DNA. Just give him time to process. He'll forgive you. Things will be … different … now."

"He'll never talk to me again." Maddie was belligerent in her beliefs.

"You need some sleep," Olivia said, resting her transparent body against Maddie's shaking frame. "Things will be better tomorrow. I promise."

Maddie didn't answer. She couldn't. Sorrow was overtaking her.

"Go to sleep, sunshine," Olivia said. "I'll be right here while you sleep. Things will be okay. Things will ... be better. Have faith. You and Nick are destined to be together. I've always known it. So has he. Just ... give him time."

Maddie's sobs didn't subside for almost an hour. Finally, as the sun moved across the horizon to initiate a new day, sleep claimed her. Only then did Olivia leave. There was another person to check on, and she loved him almost as much as he loved her daughter.

Nick's sleep was just as restless as Maddie's when Olivia popped into his bedroom. She did her best to soothe him.

"It's going to be okay," she whispered in his ear. "Things will be better now. You'll see. Don't give up on her."

"Maddie," Nick murmured, shifting in his bed and clutching his pillow desperately. "My Maddie."

Olivia smiled. "She's waiting for you."

19. NINETEEN

Maddie was more exhausted when she woke up than when she finally passed out. Olivia had left while she slumbered, and Maddie felt her void as keenly as she felt Nick's. She needed to get out of the house.

After a quick shower, Maddie let her hair air dry as she escaped out the back door. She'd heard Maude banging around on the second floor, and as much as Maddie loved her grandmother, she couldn't deal with another emotional upheaval. Not today.

Instead of heading to the lake like she normally would – she didn't want to risk someone discovering her there – Maddie hiked five miles east. If the day would've been hotter, it would've been an arduous trek. Since it was still spring, Maddie only worked up a mild sweat during the walk.

She arrived at Black Creek about two hours after she left the house, following a meandering path to her destination. While Willow Lake was where Maddie felt at home, Black Creek was where Maddie went to escape. And she needed to escape today.

Maddie was angry with herself. She should've thought of a lie to tell Nick when he started questioning her. She should've stayed away from the alley. She should've ... done something.

Maddie sank down on the ground and removed her shoes,

dipping her feet in the slow-moving creek as she stared at one of the many hidden gems Blackstone Bay had to offer. The town was an abundance of water. There was access to Lake Michigan on one side, Willow Lake on the north end of town, and Black Creek in the woods at the northeast corner of the town grid. That was on top of the fast-moving river on the west side of town. For water enthusiasts, Blackstone Bay was a dream.

So, why did Maddie feel like she was trapped in a nightmare?

"Did you hike out here alone?"

Maddie jerked her head when she heard Nick's voice. She shouldn't have been surprised to find him out here. They'd discovered the spot together while exploring as children. Since they both deemed it "magic," they only returned on special occasions. Maddie had fled to the spot for refuge today. She could only wonder if Nick had done the same. "I … just felt like walking."

Nick's face was unreadable as he studied her. After a few moments, he moved to her side and sat down next to her. He wasn't close enough to touch her, but he wasn't pulling away either. He removed his own shoes and plunged them into the cool water. "I was doing the same thing. I honestly thought I would be alone out here."

"I'm sorry," Maddie murmured. "I can go if you want." She made as if to pull her feet out of the water.

"Stay right there," Nick said. "Don't go."

Maddie's heart sank. "I … are you ready to yell at me?"

"I'm not going to yell."

"You can," Maddie said. "I think you've earned it, and I definitely deserve it."

"I'm not going to yell at you, Maddie," Nick said, irked. "Stop trying to get me to yell at you. You're only doing it because you think it will make you feel better. I'm not going to emotionally beat you up to fulfill some stupid imaginings from ten years ago."

Maddie's mouth dropped open, stunned. "That is not what I'm doing."

"That's exactly what you're doing," Nick countered. "You've spent two decades convincing yourself that I would turn on you if you told me the truth. Well, guess what? That's not what's going to happen. Now, just sit there and shut up. I'm still thinking."

"You want me to sit here and shut up?"

Nick smirked. "Do you think that's possible?"

"I … fine." Maddie snapped her mouth shut and focused on the trickling water. "You're going to miss the sound of my voice, though. You'll see."

"Shut up, Maddie."

NICK STUDIED HER PROFILE THOUGHTFULLY. Her eyes were puffy, and he had a sneaking suspicion she'd been up crying all night. Her hair was freshly washed – he could smell the faint citrus scent wafting from it – but it was straggly, like she'd run a brush through it and then forgotten about it. She wasn't wearing any makeup, but he liked her face scrubbed and bare. She still didn't look like herself.

Nick knew they needed to talk. He just wasn't sure how to start the conversation. He was determined to get everything out in the open and then move on. He'd just gotten his best friend back – even though they were still struggling. There was no way he was going to let her slink away and hide inside a cloud of self-doubt now. Enough was enough.

He finally decided to break the silence. "Did you sleep last night?"

"I thought you didn't want me to talk?"

"You can speak now," Nick teased. "I just needed a few minutes to collect my thoughts. I wasn't expecting you out here."

"I told you … ."

"You're not leaving, Maddie," Nick said. "I didn't say I wanted you to go. I said I needed a few minutes."

"You're so bossy," Maddie grumbled.

Nick sighed dramatically. "Oh, good grief. Did you sleep or not? Your face is all puffy, and you look tired."

"You look tired, too," Maddie shot back. "Did you sleep?"

"Not a lot," Nick admitted. "I tossed and turned most of the night. When I finally did get to sleep … I had a really odd dream."

Maddie's eyes widened. "Were you killing me in it?"

Nick chuckled. "No. Your mom was there, though. It wasn't really a dream. It was more like I could hear her talking to me."

"What was she saying?"

"I don't really remember," Nick said. "I just remember feeling ... comforted." Maddie bit her bottom lip, and Nick could see her mind working. "What?"

"My mom was with me for a few hours last night," she said.

Nick shifted his shoulders. "Is your mom still here?"

Maddie nodded.

"Is that why you came home? Did you know she would be here?"

"I hoped she would be here," Maddie clarified. "I came home because ... because I wanted to come home. I've wanted to come home for as long as I can remember. Mom dying was just the final straw."

"Why did she stay? I mean, does everyone stay behind?"

"No. Most people move on. Mom stayed for Granny."

Nick waited.

"Granny says that Mom won't leave until they can go together," Maddie said. "She says that a mother should never outlive her child."

"That's nice," Nick said, considering. "Do you think Olivia came to see me last night?"

"She knew I was upset," Maddie replied cagily. "I think it would be just like her to go and see you. She always loved you."

"I always loved her, too."

"Did you see her a lot after I left?"

"I had lunch with her once a week once I was back in town after the academy," Nick replied, guileless. "I would bring lunch to the store and we would just ... talk."

"Thank you for being there for her," Maddie said, sniffling as she fought back tears. "You were better to her than I was."

"I think Olivia knew you were struggling, Mad," Nick said. "She didn't hold it against you."

"Well, she gave me an earful last night," Maddie said. "It seems I might have ... misunderstood ... some of the advice she gave me."

"She expected you to tell me the truth a long time ago, didn't she?"

"I don't understand," Maddie admitted. "She drilled it into my head over and over again: Don't tell anyone your secret. When I told her what happened, she was angry because I never told you the truth."

"I'm not just anyone, Maddie," Nick said. "Olivia knew what you refused to see."

"And what was that?"

"I would never just abandon you," Nick said. "Even though that's exactly what you did to me."

Maddie's face contorted as she dropped it into her hands. "I'm so sorry."

"I know you're sorry," Nick said, fighting the urge to reach over and pull her to him. They weren't there yet. He still needed more time – and there was more to talk about. "I think you've been sorry for a really long time. That doesn't change the fact that you didn't trust me. I have to wonder what I did to make you think I would turn away from you."

"I … I just couldn't bear the thought of you not being in my life."

"So, instead, you cut me out of your life," Nick said. "That makes a lot of sense."

"I … ."

"I want us to be able to get past this, Mad," Nick said. "I'm just not sure how we're going to do it. You're obviously feeling vulnerable, and I'm still feeling … ."

"Betrayed," Maddie finished.

"Confused," Nick corrected. "While we're working our way through this, though, I need you to understand that I'm not scared by what you are. I spent hours last night thinking back … and I'm not sure how I missed it. I feel a little stupid now."

"You didn't want to see it," Maddie said. "You wanted me to be normal, like you."

"Yeah, that's not it," Nick said. "I never once thought you were normal. That's why I liked you in the first place. I never could've been friends with a normal girl."

Maddie faltered. "I'm not sure I understand."

"A normal girl plays with dolls and hates bugs," Nick said. "A normal girl cares about makeup, hair spray, and clothes. You cared about playing in the woods, and watching action movies with me. You were never normal, Maddie. You were better than that."

"So, you're saying you would've been fine with all of this if I told you back then?" Maddie's face was twisted with doubt.

"I would've been fine with it," Nick said. "It might have even been fun."

Maddie started crying again, and this time Nick couldn't resist comforting her. He shuffled over and wrapped his arms around her waist, pulling her onto his lap as her shoulders heaved against his chest.

"Don't cry, Mad," Nick said, resting his forehead against the back of her head. "I can't take it when you cry."

"I ruined everything."

"You didn't ruin anything," Nick said. "You just ... screwed it up for a decade."

Despite herself, Maddie laughed. The sound, although harsh, lifted some of the weight off Nick's shoulders.

"It's okay, Maddie," he said. "We're ... going to figure this all out."

"How?"

"Well, we're going to start over," Nick replied.

"And how do we do that?"

"We're going to start from the beginning," he said. "I want to know everything."

"Everything?"

"Everything," Nick confirmed, rubbing his hand over the back of her neck to soothe her. "You're going to tell me everything, and I'm going to listen, and then we're going to figure out how to move on from there. I'm not saying it's going to be easy, and I'm not saying everything is going to be figured out today.

"I'm not going to let you run away again, though," Nick said. "I can't take it, and I'm pretty sure it would destroy you. So, let's take the first step. When did you first talk to a ghost?"

Maddie sucked in a deep and steadying breath. Nick was worried she was going to clam up again. He was terrified she would start lying to protect herself. Instead, she launched into her story – and she didn't stop talking for hours. Nick took every step down memory lane with her, and things were ... different ... when she was done. He wasn't sure things would ever be the same, but he was almost certain they would be better.

It was a start. Now he just had to figure out what the next step was.

20. TWENTY

Nick walked Maddie back to Magicks once the sun started dipping in the west. He felt emotionally drained after their afternoon, but he also felt markedly better. Once Maddie started opening up, she didn't stop. She looked as relieved to get it off her chest as he felt to hear it.

They continued to chat during the long walk home.

"When did you know nursing wouldn't work out for you?"

"It wasn't long," Maddie said. "Hospitals are teeming with ghosts. I knew I couldn't keep ignoring them."

"And you couldn't talk to them without putting yourself at risk," Nick said, holding his hand out to help Maddie climb over a fallen tree. When she landed on the other side, he didn't let go of her hand. "You didn't think about that when you decided to be a nurse?"

"I just knew I wanted to help people," Maddie said, gripping his fingers tightly. Nick recognized the gesture. She was anchoring herself through him. It was the first time she'd done it since she returned, even though she'd always done it before, and he didn't realize how much he'd missed it until now.

"There are a lot of different ways to help people, Mad," Nick said. "You can help them right from the store. Look what you're trying to do for Jennifer."

"Speaking of Jennifer, did you really make sure Dustin took her home the other night?"

"I did," Nick said.

"That's so ... adult."

"Dustin is a little pig," Nick said. "Jennifer can do a lot better."

"Oh, you're so sweet," Maddie teased, poking the index finger of her free hand into his cheek.

Nick rolled his eyes. "I'm just saying that you can help people right here in town," he said, trying to get the conversation back on topic. "You don't need to be anything that you're not to help people. You're amazing just the way you are."

"Thank you." Maddie's face flushed.

"Is that what happened with Detective Kincaid?"

When Maddie stilled, Nick realized his mistake. While she'd been filling him with nothing but truth for hours, he was still harboring a secret.

"How do you know about him?" Maddie's voice was barely a whisper.

Nick licked his lips. "I talked to him."

"What? Why?"

"Because I was concerned about you," Nick said, cringing when Maddie snatched her hand back from his. "Maddie, you were acting strange. I caught you out in the meadow talking to yourself. I know now you were talking to Olivia, but that whole thing was odd.

"You knew Sarah's name when it hadn't been released. Then there was the thing with Sadie," he continued. "You got physically ill, Mad. You led me to her, and your cheeks were bright red, and ... I just knew something was up."

"That doesn't explain how you knew about Kincaid," Maddie said, her face ashen.

Nick was terrified to tell her the truth. He'd known it was an invasion of privacy when he was doing it, but now it felt like he was the one who had betrayed her. He couldn't do anything but tell her the truth now. "I ran your name through the system," he said. "I found quite a few hits, and all of them were in Kincaid's case files."

Maddie's hand flew to her mouth. "I ... and you called him?"

"I did," Nick said. "He's a nice guy, Mad. He had glowing things to say about you. He was worried you were a suspect in Sarah's death, and he was already thinking of ways to clear his schedule so he could come up here and help you."

"He's a good man," Maddie said finally. "I haven't seen him in a few years. How did he sound?"

Her voice was distant, and Nick couldn't help but feel a twinge of jealousy at her words. Had they been involved? "He seemed busy. He was more concerned about you."

"Well, that sounds just like him."

Nick bit the bullet. "Did you two date?"

The incredulous look that flitted across Maddie's face was almost comical. "He's in his fifties."

Nick's smile was sheepish. "Oh. I ... it was just the way you talked about him."

"Trust me. There was nothing romantic going on with Kincaid," Maddie said. "It was purely work."

Nick was relieved. "And you helped him find missing people?"

"I did," Maddie said, her jaw stiffening. "For almost two years."

"Then what happened?"

"I ... something bad."

"If you don't want to talk about it, you don't have to," Nick said quickly. "I invaded your privacy. You don't owe me an explanation."

Maddie shifted her eyes to the horizon, considering. "I'm not sure I'm ready to talk about it."

"You don't have to," Nick said carefully. "Just know that I'm here when you're ready."

"I ... it's just too horrible."

"Okay," Nick said, holding his hand out to her again. "Let's go back to the house and get Maude for some dinner. I'm starving, and I'm betting you haven't eaten in almost twenty-four hours."

"What makes you say that?"

She still hadn't taken his hand, and Nick was worried he'd created a new chasm in their relationship. "Because I know you," he said.

"Whenever you're upset, you stop eating. Most women bury themselves in ice cream and cookies. You bury yourself in working out and pouting."

"I do not."

"You do, too." Nick kept his hand outstretched. *Please, Maddie,* he internally begged. *Take it.*

Maddie slipped her hand back in his. "I don't bury myself in pouting."

Nick was so relieved when she took his hand he missed her follow-up statement. "What do you want for dinner? We could order pizza."

"That sounds fine."

They emerged from the woods behind the house, and the figure standing on the side of the driveway took Nick by surprise. "Sonovabitch."

Maddie followed his gaze. "Oh, you've got to be kidding me," she grumbled. "I thought I scared him away."

Nick's gaze was hateful when it landed on Todd. "He's still sniffing around you?"

"He showed up with a picnic the other day," Maddie admitted. "I told him I wanted a bunch of kids because I thought that would freak him out. I didn't expect to see him again. He's obsessed with you, by the way. He doesn't really want to date me. He just wants to poke you."

"I'm going to poke him with my foot in his … ."

"Nicky," Maddie warned.

Nick gripped Maddie's hand tighter as they moved closer to the house. He was sending a message, too, and that message was: Stay away.

"Well, well, well," Todd said when he caught sight of them. "I guess I should have expected this."

"Expected what?" Nick asked, ushering Maddie in front of him with a hand on her narrow waist as he navigated her past Todd. He was determined to keep Todd from touching her.

"Well, Maddie swore up and down you two were just friends, and yet here you are … holding hands." Todd's face was murderous. "I knew she was lying."

"We are just friends," Nick said, refusing to rise to the bait. "That doesn't mean we don't touch one another." He gave Maddie a little push toward the front door. "Go and order the pizza."

Maddie's face was conflicted. "What are you going to do?"

"I'm just going to have a short … discussion … with Winthrop," Nick said, fighting to keep his voice even.

"But … ."

"It will be fine, Mad," Nick said.

"Yes, it will be fine, *Mad*," Todd said, sarcasm dripping from his tongue. "Winters here just wants to make sure I understand my boundaries."

"Nicky, just … come and order the pizza with me," Maddie pleaded.

"I'll be inside in five minutes," he said, refusing to move his gaze from Todd's face. "I promise. Everything is going to be fine."

"Yeah, it's going to be great," Todd said. "We're going to toss a football and bond."

Maddie resignedly moved in the direction of the house after shooting a pointed warning look in Todd's direction. "Don't you upset him."

"I'm the one who just found his girl with another man," Todd replied. "I'm the one who is upset."

"Oh, please," Maddie scoffed. "I was never your girl. You just wouldn't take the hint."

"Well, I get it now," Todd shot back. "You're a tease."

Nick grabbed his arm roughly. "Don't talk to her like that."

Maddie paused on the porch. "Nick?"

Nick released Todd's arm and sent her a reassuring smile. "It's fine. Order the pizza. I promise things won't get out of hand."

Maddie didn't look convinced, but she disappeared inside the house anyway. Once she was gone, both men let their facades slip.

"You just couldn't let anyone else have her, could you?" Todd was angry.

"She's better than you," Nick said. "I'm just making sure you don't take advantage of her."

"Do you think she's too stupid to make her own decisions?"

Nick made a face. "I think you're too aggressive to give her much of a choice."

"You're just friends, though, right? Why do you care so much?"

"Because friends don't let friends date jerks," Nick replied. "She's not interested in you."

"That's not what she said the other day," Todd replied, smirking. "The other day she told me she wanted five kids and she thought I could provide for them very well. She wanted to get started making them right away."

Nick snorted. "Maddie only wants one kid," he replied. "She liked growing up as an only child."

Todd's smug smile slipped. "But … ."

"She was trying to scare you away," Nick said. "She figured a ladies' man like yourself would turn and run when she mentioned wanting a boatload of kids. Buy a clue."

"You're just so full of yourself," Todd said. "I'm not even sure you realize what you're doing."

"And what's that?" Nick asked, crossing his arms over his chest.

"You're claiming her as your own," Todd shot back. "You're marking your territory."

Todd's words hit home. Nick knew he was doing exactly that. He just didn't want Maddie to know it. Not yet, at least. "I'm making sure she's protected," Nick countered. "You're not good enough for her."

"And you are?"

"That's not even a consideration right now," Nick said, refusing to lose his temper. "Maddie is trying to settle back into her life here. Her mother just died. She's taking over a business for the first time. You're a distraction she doesn't need."

"Because you only want her to be distracted with you," Todd supplied.

"I want Maddie happy," Nick replied. "You're not capable of making her happy. What she needs right now is peace. You're not peaceful, Winthrop. You're like a tornado. You just want to swoop in here and upend her life. I'm not going to let you do that."

"You're such a punk," Todd seethed. "I have to ask, what does your girlfriend think about you and your *friend* spending so much time together?"

Nick hadn't given much thought to Cassidy this afternoon. To be fair, he hadn't given her much thought since ... well ... the day they started dating. It wasn't lost on Nick that he was treating the amiable teacher the same way he was worried about Todd treating Maddie. He definitely needed to address that situation – and soon. "My relationship with Cassidy is none of your concern."

"Is your relationship with Maddie any of her concern?" Todd challenged.

"Not really."

"And how does Maddie feel about you fawning all over her while your girlfriend sits at home pining over you? Or does she get off on it?"

Nick frowned. "My relationship with Cassidy is none of your business," he said. "My relationship with Maddie is none of your business. I'm sure there are a few women left in this town who are dumb enough to date you, but Maddie isn't one of them. Move on."

"And what if I don't?" Todd pressed.

"Then I'm going to make you wish you'd never laid eyes on her."

"Is that a threat?"

"It's a promise," Nick replied. "Stay away from Maddie. I'm not going to tell you again."

Todd's eyes narrowed. "You're not her father."

"I never said I was."

"You're not her boyfriend either."

"Stay away from her," Nick repeated. "You're not welcome here. Don't make me tell you again because you're not going to like it if I have to."

The sound of the front door of the store opening again caught Nick's attention. He shifted his gaze to the porch and found Maddie standing there, her hands clasped in front of her and worry furrowing between her eyebrows. "I ordered the pizza."

Neither man spoke.

"How are things going out here?" She sounded like she was about to have a meltdown.

"They're fine," Todd said, squaring his shoulders. "We were just about to build a fort."

"Yeah," Nick replied. "I'll go inside and get the pillows and you … leave." He turned his full attention to Maddie. "Did you get mushrooms on it?"

Todd had been dismissed, and he knew it. He slunk back to his car and left, his eyes never leaving Nick's back as he joined Maddie on the porch. They both seemed lost in their own little world, and Nick's victory – however small – left a bad taste in Todd's mouth.

"We're not done here," Todd muttered to himself. "We're so not done."

21. TWENTY-ONE

Maddie found Nick relaxing in the window seat a few hours later. She'd been searching through the house for him – momentarily worried he'd snuck out without telling her – and when her eyes finally landed on him, she was overwhelmed with a quick rush of relief. Part of her was still waiting for him to run.

"What are you doing in here?"

Nick raised his eyes from the book he was scanning. "Isn't this what we always used to do after dinner?" He patted the open spot next to him. "I thought we would start another book."

Maddie grinned. "You want to start reading books together again?"

"I do," Nick said, his smile lazy. "I've grown illiterate without you."

Maddie climbed up next to him. "What book did you pick?"

Nick handed it to her, and Maddie's face colored with embarrassment when she realized what he'd been flipping through. It was one of Olivia's old Harlequin romances. "We can't read this."

"Why not?" Nick asked, feigning ignorance.

"I ... you know why."

"Because you don't want to read the sex scenes out loud," Nick finished for her. "Admit it."

"You don't want to read that book either," Maddie countered. "There's no action in it."

"Oh, there's a lot of action, Mad," Nick said, poking her side suggestively. "I think it will be good for us to get back in the swing of things."

Maddie swallowed hard. *Was he flirting?* "We can't read that book because Granny is here." Maddie tried a different tactic. "She'll be scandalized."

"Maude left five minutes ago," Nick replied, arching an eyebrow. "She said she had a hot date."

Maddie was dumbfounded. "She did? I didn't hear her leave."

"That's because you were doing the dishes."

"What did she say? I didn't know she was dating anyone."

"She said she had some hot action waiting for her," Nick said, grinning. "She didn't say who, but she did have an extra pair of panties in her purse."

Maddie's mouth dropped open. "She did not!"

"She did, too," Nick said. "She showed them to me."

"You're making that up."

"Okay, maybe she didn't show them to me," Nick conceded. "She wanted to, though."

Maddie snorted. "You're incorrigible."

Nick leaned back so he could stare at the ceiling. The glow-in-the-dark stars Olivia had affixed in the small corner reminding him of a happy childhood. "Pick a book, Mad," he said. "If you're not going to read this one with me – and I'm taking it home so I can finish it, just so you know – you need to pick one."

Maddie glanced at the bookshelf next to them. "What are you in the mood for?"

Nick waved the paperback in her face again.

"I can't read that with you," Maddie said. "I'll die of shame."

"You're so cute I can't stand it sometimes," Nick said. "Grab that one."

Maddie followed his finger and pulled out the book in question. "You want to read *The Shining*?"

"I haven't read it in years," he said. "We used to love to read Stephen King together."

"Okay," Maddie said, settling into the crook of his arm. "I'm not going to be able to sleep for a week, but anything is better than *The Highlander's Conquest*."

Nick snickered. "We have to broaden your reading horizons."

"Maybe later," Maddie said, resting her head against his chest. "Do you want to go first?"

Nick took the book from her and started to read out loud. It was hard for him to concentrate with her in such close proximity, but he was determined to reintroduce normalcy into their lives.

An hour later, they'd both dropped off. Nick had covered them with a blanket, and they were lost in happy slumber, the book discarded on the floor next to them. Olivia hovered close as she watched them, a small smile playing over her lips.

"Sleep well, my lovelies," she whispered. "It won't be long now."

WHEN Nick woke the next morning, it took him a few seconds to get his bearings. The warm body next to his felt amazing and he shifted so he could wrap an arm around Maddie's waist and bury his face in her flaxen hair. Sometime in the night, they'd both turned on their sides, and Nick had spooned up against her back. Their bodies fit together like they were meant to be joined. Nick hadn't slept this well in a decade, and he wasn't ready to lose the moment.

When Maddie started to stir, Nick waited. Would she freak out? Would she pull away from him? Would she try to find distance? Instead, she rolled over and buried her face in his chest. "Morning," she murmured.

"Morning," Nick said, brushing her hair out of her face. "How did you sleep?"

"Like a rock," Maddie admitted.

"You were exhausted," Nick said. "You needed the sleep."

"This couldn't have been very comfortable for you," Maddie said. "You can't fully stretch your legs out."

"I'm fine, Mad," he said. "I slept just as hard as you did. I think I needed it, too."

"How far did we get in the book?"

"Not far," Nick said, pushing his mussed hair off his forehead. "Don't worry. We have time."

Maddie giggled when Nick's stomach chimed in with a loud growl. "Are you hungry?"

"I could eat," Nick said. "Do you want leftover pizza?"

"Yeah, we're not teenagers anymore," Maddie said. "How about I cook breakfast?"

"What did you have in mind?"

"Pancakes?"

"Sold," Nick said, internally sighing when Maddie pulled away. He was starving, but he would've been perfectly happy snuggling up with her in the window seat for the entire day.

"Do you have to work today?"

"Not until this afternoon," Nick said, following her into the hallway that led to the back of the house.

"How is your investigation going?"

"I don't really know," Nick admitted. "I'm not the primary. Kreskin is in charge."

"Does that bug you?"

"Not really," Nick said. "I'd like to be more involved, mostly for the learning experience, but I also don't mind the onus of the investigation being on someone else. I've had my hands full with … other things."

"Me," Maddie said knowingly. "I've totally screwed up your life by coming back, haven't I?"

Nick was serious as he regarded her. "No, Mad. You screwed up my life by leaving," he said. "You fixed it by coming back. Now get your butt moving. I need food, and you promised me pancakes."

"You're a lot bossier than I remember," Maddie grumbled. She pushed into the kitchen and pulled up short when she realized the small table at the end of the room wasn't empty. "What the … ?"

Nick followed her, curious. The sight that greeted him was both hilarious and horrifying. Maude had returned during the night, not waking either of them from their heavy slumber. She apparently hadn't returned alone.

"I see you two finally woke up," Maude said, adjusting her nightgown so it covered more of her thigh. "You know Henry."

The man sitting next to Maude, his robe open wide so everyone could see his sagging chest and beer gut, fixed Nick and Maddie with a wide smile. "Good morning, kids."

"Henry," Nick said, pushing Maddie forward slightly. "How is the greenhouse business?"

"It's planting season," Henry said. "You know how that goes."

"This is your busy season?"

"This and the fall," Henry said, sipping from his mug of coffee. "Thankfully, Carrie has taken over most of the day-to-day operations so I can be free to … do other things." He smiled at Maude happily.

"Carrie is a good niece," Maude said.

Nick glanced at Maddie to see how she was handling the situation. She looked like she was in shock. "Well, Maddie promised me pancakes," he said. "Are you guys hungry?"

"Oh, yeah," Henry said. "I worked up quite the appetite last night."

Nick rubbed Maddie's back soothingly. "Start cooking, Mad. You've got some hungry mouths to feed."

Maddie sent him a scorching look. "This isn't funny."

"I'm not laughing."

"You're about to."

"Fix my breakfast, woman," he ordered. "I'm going to have some coffee with Maude and Henry. This is going to be fun."

"This is … mortifying."

MADDIE BUSIED herself with breakfast as she tried to get a handle on what was happening. Maude had brought a man home. Maude had brought a man home and … . It was just too horrifying to think about.

"There are blueberries in the fridge," Maude said.

"I know," Maddie replied. "I'm the one who bought them."

"I was just reminding you," Maude said. "There's no reason to be snippy."

"I'm not snippy."

"Hey, I'm not the only one who had an overnight guest of the male persuasion," Maude pointed out.

"That's different," Maddie said. "We were just . . . ."

"Cuddling on the window seat," Maude said. "I saw you when I came in."

"Why didn't you wake us?"

"Because you needed your sleep," Maude replied. "You two were dead to the world."

"You were kind of cute," Henry agreed. "Nick was all cuddled up behind you. You couldn't even see his face because it was lost in all that hair of yours."

"I . . . ."

"And you were both snoring like freight trains," Maude added.

"I don't snore."

"You do when you're exhausted," Maude said. "And you two were both exhausted. There was no way I was waking you up. I did take pictures, though."

Maddie stilled. "What?"

"We took pictures," Henry said. "Maude wants to frame one of them."

Maddie glanced at Nick for support. He didn't seem bothered by the admission.

"I must not be much of a cop," he said. "I didn't even hear you guys come in."

"That's what happens when you run on emotional fumes for two days," Maude said. "You needed your sleep. You didn't miss work or anything, did you?"

"No. I don't have to go in until this afternoon," Nick replied. "I'm fine. I'm starving, but I'm fine."

"I'm working on it," Maddie said.

"Work faster," Nick teased.

Maude smiled at the interplay. "It's good to see things are back to normal," she said. "I saw you even had a book out."

"You two spent your night reading a book?" Henry asked, nonplussed. "You know that's not the right way to do it, don't you?"

Maddie pressed her lips together as she started mixing ingredients in a big bowl.

"Don't embarrass them," Maude chided. "They always use to curl up in that window seat and read books together. It's like foreplay for them."

"Granny!"

"Oh, get over it," Maude said, waving her hand. "You're going to be thirty in two years, Maddie. You should know what sex is before that happens."

"I can't believe this," Maddie mumbled.

Nick smiled at her from his spot at the table, although his eyes were thoughtful as he regarded her. "Yeah, Maddie."

"You're on thin ice," Maddie said, waving the spatula in his direction. "You're supposed to be on my side."

"I'm always on your side," Nick said. "You're just so dramatic sometimes."

"I am not dramatic." Maddie scanned the Bisquick box for a second. "Do we have another box of this?"

"In the pantry," Maude said.

Maddie shuffled across the kitchen floor and opened the pantry door, gasping audibly when Sarah popped into view.

"What's wrong?" Maude asked.

"Nothing," Maddie replied, recovering quickly. "I just thought I saw ... a mouse." She lowered her voice. "What are you doing here?"

"I wanted to talk to you," Sarah said. "I didn't realize you weren't alone."

"I ... it's fine to pop in when it's just Granny," Maddie whispered. "Even Nick knows now. Henry doesn't, though."

"I can come back later."

"That would probably be best."

Sarah peered around Maddie's shoulder curiously. "That's the police officer from the other night."

Maddie nodded.

"He's really hot."

Maddie nodded again.

"Is he your boyfriend?"

Maddie shook her head. This wasn't a conversation she could participate in now.

"Your grandmother is adorable."

Maddie could think of a few other words to describe her.

"Is that her boyfriend?"

"I have no idea," Maddie muttered.

"He's … ." Sarah's head shifted as she regarded Henry, and then all the color drained from her face. That was an impressive feat since Sarah no longer had blood flowing through her ethereal body.

"What's wrong?"

"I … ."

"Do you recognize him?"

"I … I have to go." Sarah blinked out of existence.

"Sarah!" Maddie was beside herself. *What just happened?*

Nick appeared at Maddie's side. "Who are you talking to?"

"I … ." Maddie glanced over her shoulder and focused on Henry.

"Is it Olivia?" Nick asked. "Tell her I said 'hi.'"

"It's wasn't Mom," Maddie murmured. "It was Sarah Alden."

Nick was intrigued. "What did she say?"

"She didn't say anything," Maddie replied. "Well, she said you were hot."

Nick smirked. "What can I say? Women love me."

"Then she saw Henry," Maddie said, her face troubled. "It was like she recognized him. Then she freaked and disappeared."

Nick followed Maddie's gaze to the table, where an enthusiastic Henry was regaling Maude with a fishing story. "Why do you think she did that?"

"I have no idea," Maddie said. "We need to find out, though. It was like she was … scared."

Nick rubbed the back of Maddie's neck thoughtfully. "Finish breakfast," he said. "We can't do anything about it now, and I don't want you to draw attention to yourself. I don't think Henry is known for being tight-lipped."

Maddie nodded.

Nick brushed a quick kiss against her forehead. It was friendly, but Maddie shivered involuntarily at his touch. "It's still okay, Mad. Everything is going to be okay."

Maddie wished she could believe him.

22. TWENTY-TWO

"Where is everyone?"

Christy looked around at her empty salon and shrugged. "It's just one of those weird lulls," she said. "I purposely try to schedule people for early in the day so I can get out at a respectable hour. This is one of the rare afternoons it worked out."

Maddie nodded, unsure. "You're not getting boycotted, are you?"

"Why would people boycott me?"

"Because of the other night."

Christy snickered. "I'm the town hero because of that," she said. "There have been no less than twenty mothers parading through here thanking me for keeping their daughters' virtue intact."

"Do they know you weren't really doing that?"

"Of course not," Christy said. "I told them I was, though. Everyone wants me to start attending church services now."

Maddie pressed her lips together. "Do you want to go to church?"

"Honey, I'm not getting up early enough on a Sunday – my one day a week that I have all to myself – to go to church," Christy replied. "They don't need to know that, though. I'm a morality crusader right now. I'm more popular than ever."

"And people aren't giving you crap about hanging out with me, right?" Maddie was worried.

"Why would they?"

"People hate me."

"You're unbelievable," Christy said. "People don't hate you."

"Marla hates me."

"Marla hates herself," Christy replied. "She's so miserable she thinks she has to make others miserable to bolster her own self-esteem. It's sad. People hate her, not you."

"She was the most popular girl in high school."

"She was the most terrifying girl in high school," Christy corrected. "She was popular because people were scared to tell her she was a horrible person. That's not really being popular."

"I remember her being popular."

"That's because you were scared to death of her," Christy said.

"She was mean to me."

"She was mean to you because she was jealous of you," Christy said.

"She was not jealous of me."

"Maddie, you have got to get a handle on the way you look at yourself," Christy said. She climbed up from the chair she was sitting on and patted it. "Sit here, please."

Maddie was leery, but she did as instructed. She'd never really had a female friend, and she was desperate to hold on to Christy. Once she was settled, she met Christy's gaze in the mirror expectantly. "Why am I sitting here?"

"I want you to tell me what you see when you look at yourself," Christy said.

"I see … me."

"Yes, but be more specific," Christy said. "What do you see when you look at your hair?"

Maddie had always considered her hair to be her best asset. "I like the color."

"The color is absolutely beautiful," Christy agreed. "People pay hundreds of dollars to get this color."

"Are you saying you don't like the cut?"

"Your hair is extremely long," Christy said. "I would cut a few inches off, but it seems to fit you. It's simple and lovely, just like you are."

Maddie was embarrassed. "Thank you," she mumbled.

"Yeah, this is what I'm talking about," Christy said. "When someone pays you a compliment, you need to accept the praise and not be ashamed of it."

"I'm not ashamed."

"You are," Christy said. She pointed back at the mirror. "What do you think when you see your own eyes?"

Maddie shrugged. "I don't know. They remind me of my mother."

Christy's face softened. "Does that make you sad?"

"Should it?"

"Well, your mom died," Christy said. "It would make me sad."

"She's still around," Maddie admitted.

"Really?" Christy's face lit up. "That's great. Oh, wow, I never even considered that. How often do you get to see her?"

"She's still trying to get control of her new … reality," Maddie said. "Once she gets stronger, she'll be able to pop in whenever she wants."

"Oh, it's like the best of both worlds."

"I'd still rather have her here. I miss being able to touch her. I'd give anything to be able to hug her again."

"Of course you would, sweetie," Christy said, instantly contrite. "That was a stupid thing to say."

Maddie shifted in the chair. "Nick knows."

Christy's face reflected surprise. "How did that happen?"

Maddie regurgitated the past few days for Christy's rampant consumption.

"That is … amazing," Christy said when she was done. "I knew he would be fine with it."

"I feel stupid," Maddie said. "I ruined both of our lives because I was so scared. If I'd just believed in him … ."

"You can't go back in time, Maddie," Christy said. "Wait, you can't, right?"

Maddie scowled. "No."

"Then you have to let it go," Christy said. "You have to put the past ... away. It sounds like Nick is trying to do just that. You have to look to the future now."

"What future?"

"You and Nick are going to get together," Christy said. "It's only a matter of time. You're obviously not going to make the first move, so it just comes down to him. When do you think he's going to rip your clothes off?"

"He has a girlfriend, Christy," Maddie argued.

"Barely."

"He still has a girlfriend. I'm not the type of woman who thinks it's okay to go after another woman's man."

Christy snorted. "He's your man. He's always been your man. Cassidy is just renting him, and I think her lease is about to expire."

Maddie bit her bottom lip. "He hasn't mentioned anything about breaking up."

"That's because he's a good guy, and he doesn't want to hurt her," Christy said. "He already would've broken up with her if you weren't in the picture."

"Why do you say that?"

"Because he's in a spot with Cassidy," Christy explained. "I'm sure she's been pressing him where you're concerned, and I'm also sure he's denied being in love with you because it hurt too much to admit the truth.

"You two have made up now," she continued. "You're on the fast track. If he dumps her now, though, Cassidy is going to attack him. She's going to be crushed, and she's going to lash out. Frankly, I'm on your side, but she has a right to lash out. She's going to be dumped like yesterday's garbage – and soon. Nick is trying to let her down easy, and by doing that, he's actually hurting her in the long run. He just needs to crush her and get it over with."

"I don't want him to crush her," Maddie said. "She's a very nice woman."

"She is," Christy agreed. "She's not his soul mate, though."

"Do you believe in soul mates?"

"I didn't until I saw you and Nick together in high school," Christy replied. "You two gave me hope."

"I'd like to believe that," Maddie admitted.

"Because you love him," Christy supplied. "It's okay. Admitting it is the first step on the road to recovery."

Maddie tilted her head, her mind busy. "I do love him."

"I know you do. Everyone in this town knows you do. Nick knows you do. Everyone in this town also knows that Nick loves you. The only one who seems to doubt that is you."

"He loves me as a friend."

"He loves you because you're his whole heart," Christy corrected.

Maddie wanted to believe that. She just couldn't. "He's got a girlfriend."

Christy sighed. "Okay, you're not ready for this," she said. "You need to take teeny little steps right now. I get that. Tell me what else is going on."

"Sarah Alden popped into my pantry this morning."

Christy was intrigued. "What did she want?"

"She wanted to talk."

"What did she say?"

"We couldn't talk," Maddie said. "We weren't alone."

"Maude knows what you are, and now Nick knows what you are, so why couldn't you talk?"

"Granny had an ... overnight guest."

Christy waited.

"It was Henry Dunham."

"Omigod." Christy was laughing so hard tears started forming in her eyes. "I had no idea they were dating."

"I'm not sure they're dating," Maddie said. "I think they're just .... "

"Doing it?"

"I'm appalled."

"Why?" Christy was curious. "Maude is an adult. It's not like she's going to get pregnant and you're going to get stuck with a wailing infant. Why do you care?"

"I just don't want to picture my grandmother doing … that."

"No one does," Christy said. "It's still funny."

"He was wearing a robe and I could see his … chest."

"Gross," Christy said, laughing. "Was it freaky?"

"He didn't seem to care," Maddie said. "He kept telling Nick and me that we were doing it wrong."

"You are," Christy said. "That's beside the point, though. You know he wears hearing aids, right? He probably didn't know you were even talking to someone in the pantry."

"Sarah was … odd," Maddie said.

"She's dead, what do you expect?"

"She was fine at first," Maddie said. "She said Granny was cute, and she thought Nick was hot."

"He's smoking."

"When she saw Henry, though, it was as if she was looking at a ghost."

"The ghost looked like she was seeing a ghost? That had to be freaky."

"I asked her what was wrong, but she just kind of … blinked out."

"Do you think she was afraid of Henry?" Christy asked, confused. "He's harmless. The man runs a greenhouse, for crying out loud. He spends his days ordering his daughter around and pruning trees. It's not like he's a threat."

"Well, Sarah isn't from Blackstone Bay," Maddie said. "The fact that she seemed to recognize Henry worries me."

"Do you think your grandmother is sleeping with a murderer?"

Maddie shrugged. "I have no idea," she said. "I have trouble believing Henry is strong enough to kill a healthy young woman."

"I agree with that," Christy said. "Most ten-year-olds could take Henry without working up a sweat. He's a nice guy, but he's not exactly threatening."

"Maybe she recognizes him from somewhere else."

"Or maybe she recognizes him because of someone who works at the greenhouse," Christy suggested.

"I hadn't considered that," Maddie said, running her finger over her bottom lip. "Maybe Sarah was out at the greenhouse before she died. Maybe she saw Henry there. That doesn't mean he did anything to her."

"Exactly."

"Do you know who works at the greenhouse these days?"

"I know Carrie is in charge," Christy said, referring to Henry's niece. "You said it's definitely a man who killed Sarah, though, right?"

"That's what she said."

"They have seasonal help," Christy said thoughtfully. "It changes from month to month."

"Do you think we can find out who is working out there?"

Christy pursed her lips. "There's only one way I know."

Maddie was interested. "What?" Christy's smile was mischievous, and Maddie immediately regretted asking the question. "Oh, no, what are we going to do?"

"It will be fun," Christy said. "I promise."

Maddie had her doubts, but she didn't have a lot of options. "Okay. Let's do it."

23. TWENTY-THREE

"We look like idiots."

"Your hair is poking out of your hat," Christy said, slumping her shoulders as she peered over the steering wheel of her car. "Your hair is too light. You have to tuck all of it under your hat. They'll see us if you don't."

"How did you manage to find two black-knit hats in your salon?" Maddie asked, shoving her hair under the fabric. "That's just weird."

The women were parked outside Blackstone Greenhouse, and they were studying the parking lot with interest and anticipation. They were supposed to be incognito – but it wasn't going well.

Maddie had insisted on Christy driving – again – but only because she was terrified they would get caught. She didn't want anyone to report her vehicle at the scene. She knew Nick was on duty, and she'd never be able to live down the shame of her car being sighted at the greenhouse.

"We have brutal winters here," Christy said, not ruffled in the least. "You need a hat to make sure you don't get pneumonia."

"There are cuter hats."

"Oh, get over it," Christy said. "I'm not a bank robber. Why do you care?"

"I'm not sure."

"It's because you're too worried about what other people think," Christy said. "It's annoying."

"I'm sorry."

"See, you're sitting over there worried I'm thinking bad thoughts about you because you made fun of the hats," Christy said. "I'm not, by the way. Just suck it up."

"You're kind of mean," Maddie said. "I don't remember you being mean."

"I'm not mean," Christy countered. "I'm just honest."

"Brutally honest."

"That's not a bad thing."

"I didn't say it was."

"You're so cute sometimes I want to pinch your cheek." Christy did just that. "You're like a little doll. You're never mean to anyone."

"How is that a bad thing?" Maddie protested.

"It's not," Christy said. "You need to learn to stand up for yourself, though."

"I stand up for myself."

"No, you don't," Christy argued. "You let people walk all over you."

"I do not."

"Oh, please," Christy scoffed. "Do you know what your problem is?"

"I have a feeling you're about to tell me."

"Your biggest problem is that Nick has always fought your battles," Christy said. "He's so protective of you he did you a disservice."

"Nick is a wonderful man."

"Of course he is," Christy said. "That doesn't mean fighting all of your battles was a good idea. It emotionally crippled you."

Maddie shifted her head so she was facing the passenger window. "I'm not emotionally crippled."

"Maddie, Nick insisted on making sure you were safe," Christy said. "That's not a bad thing. That's why every girl in high school was desperate to climb into his pants. You're just so ... scared of fighting with people."

"I fight with people."

"No, you don't," Christy said. She pointed out the front window. "There's Joel Tarrington."

"What do you know about him?"

"He's married and ... boring," Christy said. "He's got five kids under the age of ten. He's always with them. I doubt he has the time to stalk and kill women."

"I don't remember him."

"He moved to town about five years ago," Christy said. "He's married to Katie Hubbard."

"She was a few years ahead of us, right?"

Christy nodded. "Joel is pretty henpecked. On one hand, I think that could mean he's a volcano ready to erupt. On another, he seems pretty happy being henpecked."

Maddie studied the man's slim frame. "He doesn't look very threatening."

"He's not. The three teenagers we've seen haven't looked very threatening either, though."

"Maybe this was a waste of time."

"It's only a waste of time if someone else dies because we weren't doing our job," Christy said, her eyes flashing. "Focus on the prize, Maddie. We need to make sure no one else is murdered. If we're ruling out suspects, we're doing our job."

"You're very task oriented."

"You have to be when you run your own business," Christy said. "You'll find that out once Magicks is open again."

"It's open."

"Barely," Christy said. "You've been more interested in Nick than business."

"I have not."

"That's not a bad thing," Christy said hurriedly. "You need to settle things with Nick. You're stuck until you do."

"They're settled."

"Oh, girl, things are so far from settled with Nick you should be looking to build your own little house on the prairie. It's okay. Things are going to work out."

"I don't want to keep having this argument," Maddie said. "Nick and I are friends."

"Of course you are."

"He has a girlfriend."

"For now."

"He's not interested in me romantically," Maddie pressed.

"He wants you so bad he's going to give himself a heart attack if he doesn't make a move soon," Christy said. "Huh, there's Michael Corbett. I didn't know he was working out here."

Maddie shifted her gaze. "He was a year behind us, right?"

"Right."

"What do you know about him?"

"Not a lot," Christy admitted. "He left town after graduation and joined the Army. I don't think he's dating anyone. The rumor is that he's gay, but I don't know if that's true. People keep saying it because he doesn't date, but I think he's just trying to find himself."

"He's attractive," Maddie said after studying him for a moment.

"He's very attractive."

Maddie snickered. "Are you attracted to him?"

Christy faltered. "I ... he's just a nice guy."

"Oh, you totally have a crush on him," Maddie teased. "Why don't you ask him out?"

"Why don't you ask Nick out?"

Maddie scowled. "Why do you keep doing that?"

"Because I'm not going to rest until you and Nick admit your feelings," Christy said. "You're my project now."

"I am not a project."

"No, you're work."

"I ... what the ... ? Crap." The sight of police lights flaring to life behind Christy's car filled Maddie with dread.

"Someone must have called them and said we were spying,"

Christy said, shifting her attention over her shoulder. "Is Nick on duty tonight?"

Maddie nodded.

"Well, this will be fun."

NICK CLIMBED out of his police cruiser and frowned. He recognized Christy's car, and he also recognized the blonde sitting in the passenger seat. *What are they doing?"*

Nick strode up to the driver's side of the car and knocked on the window.

Christy rolled it down and fixed him with an innocent look. "Can I help you, officer?"

"I got a call," Nick said, fighting the urge to smile. "Someone said there were two grown women out here ogling the teenage boys."

"Oh, that's such crap," Christy said. "We weren't ogling the teenage boys. They wish we were ogling them."

"They wish?"

"Cougars are very popular now."

Nick smirked. "What are you two doing out here?"

"I'm thinking of doing some gardening," Maddie interjected lamely.

"Try again."

"I … ." Maddie was lost.

"We're spying on the workers," Christy supplied. "Maddie is convinced Sarah Alden's ghost reacted to Henry because she recognized him. We both agree he's too weak to take on a healthy woman in her prime, but boffing Maude on a nightly basis is totally in his wheelhouse, so we're trying to decide if one of his workers is a killer."

Nick nodded, fighting the mad urge to laugh. "I see. Did you find anyone worth suspecting?"

"No," Christy said.

Nick leaned down so he could focus on Maddie. "Are you freaking out?"

"No."

"We're working on her self-esteem," Christy said. "I made her look at herself in the mirror at the salon for fifteen minutes earlier. I'm starting to get frustrated with her."

Nick considered the statement. "What do you mean?"

"Listen, no offense to you, but you've fought all of her battles up until this point," Christy said. "She's scared. She also thinks she's unattractive, which freaks me out because she could be a model. It's great you want to fight for her, but she needs to be able to tell people to 'eff' off."

Nick agreed with part of the statement. "She's sweet."

"She is," Christy said. "She's also an easy target. Marla is going to keep torturing her until Maddie decides she's ready to fight back."

"I can handle Marla," Nick said.

"That's part of the problem," Christy countered. "Maddie needs to learn how to fight." She looked Nick up and down, contemplating. "She needs to learn how to stake her claim."

Nick faltered. "Her claim on what?"

"What she wants."

Nick wanted to pretend he didn't know what Christy was referring to, but it was impossible. "What does she want to claim?"

Christy smirked. "Happily ever after." She pointed to the greenhouse. "Do any of those guys strike you as sociopaths?"

Nick licked his lips. He was interested in pressing Christy on the first issue, but he knew it was the worst possible time. "No. It's a mixture of teenagers and guys trying to scratch out a living. None of them seem especially dangerous to me."

"Me either," Christy said. "Sarah Alden had to react to Henry for a reason, though."

"You seem fine with this ... ghost thing," Nick said.

"I always suspected," Christy said. "I saw her talking to the air in the cemetery when we were in high school. It just made sense." She looked Nick up and down. "You seem to be adjusting well."

"She's the best friend I've ever had," Nick replied, hesitant. "I believe anything she tells me."

"And things are starting to slip into place for you," Christy interjected. "You're looking at your past and realizing what you missed. It's kind of cute."

"You guys know I'm sitting right here, don't you?"

Nick smiled at Maddie, his mind traveling to earlier in the day when he'd woken up next to her. "Christy is right," he said finally. "You need to work on your self-esteem. I haven't done you any favors in that department."

"My self-esteem is fine."

"No, it isn't," Nick argued. "You're the most beautiful person in the world, and yet you don't see it. We have time."

"That's what I've been telling her," Christy said.

A pair of headlights flashed in the parking lot as a vehicle pulled in. Maddie shifted forward, recognition washing over her face. "That's Todd's car."

"Yeah," Nick said. "Henry is his uncle. Don't ever get in that car again, by the way."

Maddie and Christy exchanged a look, and then Maddie turned to him. "I forgot about that. About Henry being Todd's uncle, I mean."

"So?"

"Todd is sexually aggressive," Maddie said.

Nick stilled. "Did he try to force you to do something?"

"Oh, get over it," Christy said. "Maddie is pointing out that Todd has ties to Henry, and Sarah Alden freaked out when she saw Henry. Maybe Todd is the one who killed Sarah."

Nick mulled the suggestion over. He'd always hated Todd – with a passion – but he'd never considered the possibility that Todd could be a murderer. "We can't jump to conclusions."

"We also can't ignore the obvious," Christy said. "Todd is one of those guys who won't take no for an answer."

"Why do you think I didn't want him around Maddie?"

Christy rolled her eyes. "Because you want Maddie for yourself," she replied honestly. "That's neither here nor there, though."

Nick straightened uncomfortably. "Why would Sarah Alden know both Henry and Todd?"

"Because she came here for some reason," Maddie mused. "I need to talk to her again."

"Is there a way you can just make her show up?"

Maddie shook her head. "It has to be her decision."

"Well, then we're stuck," Nick said. "We have no reason to follow him, and we have no reason to question him."

"His relationship with Maddie makes it doubly difficult for you, doesn't it?" Christy asked. "You can't go after him until you have really good information. If you do it now, his lawyer will just argue you have a vendetta because of your feelings for Maddie."

Nick was uncomfortable. "We don't have enough to pursue him as a suspect."

"Good grief," Christy muttered. "Between the two of you – and your refusal to admit you have feelings for one another – I'm going to develop an ulcer."

"We're friends," Maddie protested.

"We're friends," Nick agreed.

"And I'm super model," Christy said. "I just ... I'm going to lock you both in a room and steal all of your clothes. I can only take so much."

Maddie and Nick were both mortified.

"It's like babysitting without getting paid," Christy continued. "It's just ... you two both need to grow up."

Nick wanted to argue, but her point was clear. He couldn't argue with her, because he knew she was right. "I'll run a search on Todd," he said, straightening.

"Well, it's something," Christy said. "You two are still morons."

24. TWENTY-FOUR

After watching the action at Blackstone Greenhouse for another ten minutes, Nick instructed Maddie to climb into the cruiser so he could taxi her home. Maddie was worried he was going to lecture her, so she was reticent to ride with him, but Christy didn't give her a lot of options.

"Maybe he'll teach you how to steam up the windows," Christy suggested. "I think you're long past learning what that's supposed to be like."

Maddie shot her a look as she slipped into the passenger seat of Nick's cruiser. "You're not funny."

"I think she's funny," Nick said as he slid into his own seat and started the car.

"I know why the windows were steamed up."

"I'm sure you do."

"She acts like I'm ten."

"That's because she can't believe anyone could be as cute and innocent as you are," Nick teased.

Maddie's face flushed. "I'm surprised you're not yelling at me."

"Why would I yell at you?"

"Because we were out spying on the guys at Blackstone Greenhouse. I figured that would tick you off."

Nick tilted his head to the side, considering. "Do I yell at you a lot?"

Maddie faltered. "No."

"So, why did you think I would yell at you now?"

"I don't know," Maddie hedged. "We were trying to ascertain if a murderer was working out here. That doesn't particularly seem smart."

"If you had decided one of them was a murderer, what would you have done?" Nick's face was unreadable as he navigated through the Blackstone Bay streets.

"Called you."

"Maddie, the only time I'm going to be angry with you is if you lie or purposely put yourself in danger," Nick said. "From what I can tell, you and Christy were sitting in a car and gossiping. It's not like you can really tell who a murderer is just by looking at him."

"I think it's Todd."

Nick smirked. "I think you want it to be Todd. If it's Todd, you won't have to keep coming up with excuses to turn him down."

"I don't need excuses," Maddie replied. "He makes my skin crawl."

"Good," Nick said. "I don't like him being around you."

"Because he's a jerk?"

"That's one of the reasons, yes," Nick said.

"What's the other?"

Nick ignored the question. "Let's look at this from an unbiased point of view," he said. "What would Todd's motive be?"

"I think he hates women."

"Why?"

"He obviously thinks he's above them," Maddie said. "He talks about women like they're nothing more than commodities or things to barter."

"Be more specific."

"Well, when we were out on our date … ."

Nick scowled.

"He kept trying to get me to drink wine, even though I told him it went to my head and made me feel fuzzy," Maddie said. "He seemed to like that, though."

"Of course he did," Nick said. "If he got you drunk, you would've been more pliable."

"It wasn't just that," Maddie said. "He kept insisting I eat lobster because it was the most expensive thing on the menu. He kept talking about buying me the most expensive meal – even though I don't even really like lobster."

"Maybe he just wanted you to be beholden to him," Nick suggested. "Isn't there some dating myth out there that if you order the most expensive thing on the menu you have to put out?"

Maddie shrugged. "I haven't done a lot of dating. I'm not up on the rules."

"You didn't date a lot ... when you were away?" Nick was curious, despite himself.

"No."

"How come?"

"Because I just don't connect well with others," Maddie replied, her gaze focused outside the window. "The doctors at the hospital kept asking me out, but all they wanted to do was talk about themselves. I didn't trust them enough to talk about myself, so nothing really ever went anywhere."

"Well, you're better than them anyway, Mad," Nick said. "And I don't think you have problems connecting with people. We're connected, and you've connected with Christy. You just need to stop fixating on the way things should be, and start focusing on how you want them to be."

"How did you suddenly get so wise?" Maddie asked.

"I've always been wise," Nick said. "You just weren't around to see me mature into a genius."

"Ah, well, at least I know now."

Nick grinned as he pulled into Maddie's driveway. He stopped her from exiting the cruiser with a small touch, and a serious expression. "Listen, Mad. I'm not saying you're wrong about Todd," he said. "I've always hated that guy. That's why I want to think it's him. I'm worried that I'm blinding myself to the real culprit, though."

"So, what are you saying?"

"I'm saying that I want you to be careful," Nick said. "No running around at night by yourself, okay? I don't care if you have a ghost with you or not."

Maddie opened her mouth to argue.

"Don't, Mad," Nick said. "I'm not joking. I couldn't bear it if something happened to you. I want you to promise me you'll be careful."

"I promise," Maddie murmured.

"I'm going to run a check on Todd and the workers out at the greenhouse," Nick said. "I think you might be on to something."

"How are you going to explain that?"

"What do you mean?"

"We have absolutely nothing to explain our actions," Maddie said. "We have a ghost in a pantry who had a bad reaction to the old man who is sleeping with my grandmother."

Nick chuckled. "Yeah, they're kind of a cute couple."

"You're not funny."

"I'm a little funny," Nick said. "If Sarah had a bad reaction to Henry, there has to be a reason why."

"You're taking a whole lot on faith here," Maddie pointed out. "You're basing all of your actions on the fact that I say I can see ghosts. Have you asked yourself if I'm telling the truth? Have you asked yourself if I'm crazy?"

"No," Nick said. "I trust you, Mad. I believe in you. I know you're ... struggling ... with having faith in me right now, but it's going to be okay."

"I have faith in you," Maddie protested.

"In the back of your mind, you still think I'm going to run away from you," Nick countered. "I saw the look on your face last night when you found me in the window seat. You thought I'd snuck out. I'm not going to sneak out, and I'm not going to abandon you. The sooner you realize that, the better we'll all be."

"I do believe," Maddie said, biting her lip.

Nick ran his hand down the back of her head, the need to comfort her overwhelming him. "I think you want to believe," he said. "You'll get to the other part. Don't worry. Now, go in the house and lock the doors."

"You don't think Todd would follow me here, do you?"

"I don't want you to convince yourself that it's Todd until we actually know it's Todd," Nick said. "If you do that, you aren't going to be paying proper attention to your surroundings. So, as far as you're concerned, Todd is innocent. Got it?"

Maddie nodded. "Got it."

"Okay," Nick said. "Go in the house and lock the doors. Oh, and you might want to have a conversation with Maude about her bed buddy. Try to dissuade her from having him over until this thing is solved, okay?"

"Oh, yeah, that will be easy," Maddie grumbled.

Nick smiled. "If Sarah pops back up, call me on my cell phone."

"Okay."

"Maddie … ."

Maddie was halfway out of the car, but she bent back down so she could see his face.

"If you need me for anything, don't hesitate to call," Nick said. "I'll come to you no matter what."

"You always do." She shut the door.

"And I always will," Nick muttered. He waited until she was safely inside of the house before he drove away. He had some thinking to do, and despite what he'd told Maddie, he was intrigued with the idea of Todd as a suspect.

"GRANNY?"

"How many times have I told you not to call me that?"

Maddie found Maude nursing a cup of tea in the kitchen. "What should I call you?"

"Goddess Divine."

"Well, maybe on your birthday." Maddie sat down at the table and poured her own cup of tea. She raised her eyebrows when Maude slipped a bottle of bourbon out of her robe pocket and passed it across the table. "Ah, I see you weren't just drinking tea."

"I'm trying to relax before bed."

"And will you be sleeping alone tonight?"

"Will you?" Maude challenged.

"Granny, nothing happened," Maddie said, her cheeks coloring. "We just fell asleep."

"And then cuddled up like two bugs in a rug."

"I've never understood that expression."

"It's a stupid one," Maude agreed.

"I need you to do something for me," Maddie said. "I need you to put the brakes on your relationship with Henry, at least for a few days."

"I'm an adult, Maddie girl," Maude said. "I can see who I want."

"I know that," Maddie said. "It's just ... Sarah Alden was in the pantry this morning."

"Who is Sarah Alden?"

"She's the woman whose body I found the other day."

"Oh," Maude said, her eyes thoughtful. "I heard you talking. I figured you were just talking to your mother."

"No," Maddie said. "It was Sarah, and she had a bad reaction to Henry."

"What do you mean?"

Maddie described the incident.

"You don't really think Henry is capable of killing a young woman in her prime, do you?" Maude asked. "He's so out of shape he can't even be on top. His knees are shot."

"Thank you for that visual."

"I'm just saying that Henry is not capable of hurting anyone," Maude said.

"I tend to agree with you," Maddie replied. "What if Sarah recognized Henry because he was close to the person who did kill her, though?"

"Like someone out at the greenhouse?"

Maddie shrugged. "We went out there to have a look around tonight," she said. "Christy doesn't think anyone working there is capable of murder."

"What do you think?"

"I think I'd forgotten that Todd was Henry's nephew."

Maude stilled. "I kind of forgot that, too. Was he out there tonight?"

"He was," Maddie said. "He pulled up when the greenhouse was closing, and he went inside. He was still there when we left."

"Todd doesn't strike me as the type of man who does a lot of gardening," Maude mused. "I'm pretty sure he lives in one of those townhouses across Jefferson. He wouldn't even be responsible for doing his own yard work."

"Maybe he was just visiting his uncle?"

"Maybe," Maude said. "Henry never mentions him, though. I've never gotten the impression they were very close."

"Well, I just want you to be careful," Maddie said. "Nick is running a background check on Todd and everyone else out at the greenhouse."

"What if none of them are responsible?"

"I don't know," Maddie admitted. "We just have to wait for Sarah to show up again. I think she's remembering. She's the only one who can fill in the details."

Maude patted the top of the table. "Hand me my bourbon."

"I think you've had enough."

"Hey, if I'm not going to be getting any, I need to get my jollies somewhere."

Maddie frowned. "That is … ." She didn't get the chance to finish her sentence. Suddenly, all of the lights in the house blinked out and plunged Maddie and Maude into darkness – and unseen danger.

25. TWENTY-FIVE

"What's going on?"

"I don't know," Maddie said, her eyes narrowing as she tried to peer into the dark. "Maybe a fuse blew."

"That wouldn't explain the lights in the whole house going out."

Maddie's skin was tingling, which meant danger. Unfortunately, she was the one in danger this time. "We have to get out of here."

"Do you think someone is in the house?"

"Where is the circuit breaker?"

"In the garage."

"I think someone is in the garage," Maddie said. "I think they'll be in the house soon." She moved around the table so she could touch her grandmother. "We need to get out of this house. If we stay, we'll be trapped."

"You need to run, Maddie girl," Maude said. "I'll just slow you down."

"I'm not leaving you."

"You have to."

"I won't." Maddie gripped Maude's hand and started to feel around the back wall. "We'll go out through the back and circle around to the front. My car is in the driveway. I still have the keys in my pocket."

"You won't make it if you insist on taking me."

"We're either both leaving or we're both staying," Maddie said, her voice firm. "Which way is it going to be?"

Maude sighed. "We're both going. When this is over, though, I'm going to beat you upside your head."

"I can't wait."

NICK STUDIED his computer screen wearily. It was like he was going around in circles. He'd run a search on every employee at the greenhouse, and there were no red flags in any of the files.

When he'd ran Henry's name, however, something worrisome popped up. It appeared Henry hadn't always been a simple greenhouse operator. In his twenties, he'd been arrested for stalking a woman – even though they didn't call it stalking back then. The woman in question, Helen Glass, claimed Henry kept showing up outside of her classes at a mid-Michigan community college, and he'd also taken to showing up at her home. He made unwanted romantic overtures, and when Helen balked, Henry allegedly became more and more aggressive – even appearing in her bedroom one night. That's when he was arrested.

Henry was eventually convicted on misdemeanor nuisance charges and sent to the Bay County Jail for sixty days. By the time he was released, Helen Glass had moved. Since that was before information was readily available online, she'd been able to disappear, and Henry had limited options for following.

Still, Nick reasoned, stalking a woman when you're in your twenties is vastly different than killing one when you're in your seventies. He was convinced Henry didn't have the physical stamina to take a healthy woman in her twenties on. The autopsy report on Sarah Alden showed possible signs of sexual assault, but if someone raped her, they wore a condom and did no visible damage. She'd been strangled into unconsciousness at one point, and then stabbed four times in the torso. That seemed like a lot of work for an older man with knee problems.

Nick leaned back in his chair and rolled his neck. He considered calling Maddie to check on her, something in his stomach tightened when he thought of her. It wasn't the usual butterflies that flitted to and fro when he pictured heart-shaped face, though. This was something different. He just couldn't put his finger on it.

The sound of his office door opening jolted him, and when he glanced up, he was fully expecting to see Maddie for some reason. She'd been invading his thoughts all night. The woman standing there was not the one he anticipated, and he couldn't hide the feeling of disappointment as it washed over him.

"What are you doing here?"

"IT'S TOO DARK out here to see anything," Maude whispered, rubbing her knee ruefully after accidentally banging it into the siding.

Maddie had managed to get her grandmother out of the house, and they'd skirted the exterior wall until they reached the west side. Maddie could see the front driveway now, and her car was only fifty feet away. There was still an open expanse to traverse, and Maddie and Maude would be vulnerable when they tried to cross. That was Maddie's biggest concern. They had no way of no knowing where the intruder was. They had no way of knowing if he'd heard them escape and followed. They were essentially stuck.

"What are we waiting for?" Maude asked, antsy.

"I don't like how quiet it is out here."

"Would you prefer to hear the sounds of someone creeping through the bushes in our direction with a knife?"

Maddie shuddered. "Thank you for that visual."

"I'm just trying to help."

"Well, you're doing a great job of it." Maddie stepped away from the house and looked in both directions. The wind had picked up, and it was starting to rustle the leaves in the nearby trees, causing the boughs to shift and cast eerie shadows on the ground.

"Where is your cell phone?" Maude asked.

"It's on the table by the front door."

"Well, that's a great place for it."

"Where is yours?" Maddie challenged.

"In my purse." Maddie waited. "Which is on my bed."

"Do you really want to start pointing fingers here?" Despite herself, Maddie found comfort in Maude's crankiness.

"We can't just stand here, Maddie," Maude pressed. "You have to make a choice."

Maddie nodded, sighing. "Let's start for the car."

Maddie and Maude clasped hands before emerging. Maddie continued to scan every direction as she pushed Maude in front of her. The most important thing was getting Maude to the car.

They were within twenty feet when a figure detached from the east side of the house. It was too dark to make out any features, but Maddie's lungs momentarily ceased working when she saw the silhouette.

"Granny, you have to drive to the police station," Maddie hissed.

"What?" Maude was confused.

Maddie pulled the keys from her pocket and pressed them into Maude's hand. "You have to get to Nick."

"What are you talking about?"

Maddie took a step away from her grandmother, never letting her eyes drift from the still figure in front of the garage. "I'm going to lead him away from you, Granny."

When Maude finally saw what Maddie was looking at, she was appalled. "You most certainly are not."

"We don't have a choice, Granny," Maddie said. "He can cut us off before we reach the car. He's going to have to make a choice, and I'm guessing he's going to go after me instead of you."

"What makes you think that?"

"Just ... something inside of me," Maddie said, taking another step away. "Go straight to Nick and tell him what happened. He'll know how to find me."

"You're going to run into the woods, aren't you?" Maude was resigned.

"Yes."

"You could trip, Maddie," Maude argued. "If you trip, he'll catch you."

"I know the woods, Granny," Maddie said. "I'll be fine. He could trip, too. I have a better chance of hiding out there than he does of finding me."

"Maddie ... please come with me."

"I need you to be safe, Granny," Maddie said, taking another step back in the direction they'd come from. "You're all I have left."

"And you're all I have left."

Maddie couldn't risk a look at her grandmother. She couldn't take her eyes off the figure. It was starting to move in her direction, and while Maddie still couldn't make out any features, the shadow was clearly male. Broad shoulders and strong thighs gave him away. "Go now, Granny."

"Maddie ... ."

"Go!"

Maddie turned on her heel and booked back around the side of the house. She glanced over her shoulder once, long enough to make sure the man was following her and not focused on Maude. When she saw him round the corner at a run, Maddie increased her pace and plunged into the woods behind the house. She could only hope Maude would make it to Nick. She couldn't help her now.

"THAT'S NOT A VERY nice way to greet your girlfriend," Cassidy said, her face reflecting hurt. "Especially when she brought you a special dinner because you were working so late."

Nick tempered his attitude. Why did she just keep showing up? That was a stupid question. He knew why. She felt him slipping away. She didn't realize he'd already been gone for weeks.

"I'm sorry," Nick said, his tone level. "I'm just really busy. I wasn't expecting anyone to come here tonight."

"Then why did you look excited when I opened the door and then disappointed when you realized it was me?"

"I wasn't excited," Nick said. "I was ... surprised."

"I think you thought it was Maddie," Cassidy said firmly.

"I actually knew it wasn't Maddie," Nick replied. "I dropped her off at her house about an hour ago." He had no idea why he said it. Part of him was hoping Cassidy would take the admission as an attack and dump him. The truth was, he always tried to antagonize the women he dated into dumping him. That way he didn't feel like an ass when he was ready for the relationship to end. He'd been pushing Cassidy toward that same outcome for weeks – long before Maddie returned – but she refused to pull the trigger and end things. Nick was slowly coming to realize he was going to have to be the bad guy.

"You were with Maddie tonight?" Cassidy's voice was shrill. "I thought you were working?"

"I am working," Nick said. "I got a call that there was a strange car out at Blackstone Greenhouse. When I got there, it was Christy and Maddie. I needed to talk to Maddie, so I took her home."

"And last night? Where were you last night?"

Nick furrowed his brow. "What do you mean?"

"You never went home."

"Are you spying on me?" Nick was angry. He knew he'd created the situation, and he was steadfastly making it worse, but the idea that Cassidy thought she had the right to watch his house was beyond annoying.

"I went out there to see if we could spend some time together," Cassidy said, her lower lip jutting out. "You never came home."

"I fell asleep at Maddie's house," Nick said, refusing to lie. "We had a long day, and then we ordered some pizza. I was exhausted, and I fell asleep."

"Well, at least you're finally admitting you're sleeping with Maddie," Cassidy spat.

"I didn't sleep with Maddie." Well, technically he had slept with her. He knew that Cassidy was referring to sex, though. "We fell asleep."

"In her bed?"

"No, in the window seat. We used to read there all the time, and that's what we were doing when I fell asleep." Nick had no idea why he was explaining his actions. Well, that wasn't entirely true. He was doing it so Cassidy wouldn't spread rumors about Maddie when the end finally came. It didn't escape his attention that he was more worried about how his breakup with Cassidy would hurt Maddie than how it would wound Cassidy.

"We can't keep doing this," Cassidy said, running a hand through her long waves as she shifted.

Finally, Nick thought. *She's going to dump me.*

"I think we should go to couples' counseling."

Nick's mouth dropped open. "I'm sorry. I don't think I understand what you're saying."

"I love you, Nick," Cassidy said. She waited for a response, but Nick didn't give her one. That didn't stop her from plowing forward. "I think we need to talk about our issues in a formal setting, and with a professional."

"I don't have any issues," Nick said. "You clearly do, but I don't."

"All you have are issues," Cassidy said. "You know, when I started dating you, people warned me off."

"Maybe you should've listened to them."

"People told me you were pining for the great lost love of your life," Cassidy continued. "They said you were stuck in time because of some woman named Maddie Graves."

"Leave Maddie out of this," Nick snapped.

"I can't," Cassidy said. "I think her return has ... confused you. The Nick I know is sweet and caring. The Nick I know cares for me – even if he won't say it. The Nick I know would never be led around by a woman, and yet that's exactly what you're letting Maddie do to you."

"You don't know what you're talking about," Nick said, tension building in his shoulders as he fought to keep from flying off the handle.

"Well, I still think we need to talk out our issues," Cassidy said. "I want you to agree to counseling."

The time was here. Nick knew he couldn't let this go on a second longer. He searched his mind for a way to let her down easily, but everything he mulled sounded mean. Maybe there was no way around that? He opened his mouth to speak, but the cracked office door suddenly flew open to allow Maude entrance.

She was gasping for breath, and her face was clouded with color. Nick jumped to his feet. "What's wrong?"

"We're in the middle of something here, Maude," Cassidy said, petulant. "I'm sure whatever drama you've whipped up with Harriet can be postponed for a few minutes."

Maude ignored her as she fought to catch her breath. "It's Maddie."

"What happened to Maddie?" Nick's heart flopped. "Is she okay?"

"Someone came to the house," Maude said. "They cut the power. We tried to get out."

"Why isn't she with you?" Nick was furious.

"Because ... when we got to the front lawn ... he was there." Maude was beside herself, and tears started spilling down her cheeks.

Nick checked his anger. "I don't understand why she didn't come with you."

"I couldn't move fast enough," Maude said. "She led him away to give me a chance to get to the car."

Nick reached into his desk drawer and pulled out his gun, determined. "Where did she run, Maude?"

"She said you would know where to find her." Maude was sobbing.

"Willow Lake," Nick said, striding toward the door. He stopped long enough to give Maude a brief hug. "I'll find her. I'll keep her safe."

"Excuse me, Nick," Cassidy said. "You and I were having a discussion."

"Stay here, Maude," Nick ordered. "I'll bring Maddie to you as soon as I can. Call Kreskin and tell him what happened. Tell him to bring as many men to the lake as he can."

Maude nodded.

"I won't let anyone hurt her," Nick said. "I promise."

26. TWENTY-SIX

Maddie raced through the woods, internally thanking her inner intuition that she'd thought to dress in tennis shoes earlier in the evening. This trek would've been virtually impossible in sandals or flip-flops.

She knew where she was heading, but she'd decided to take a circular route to get there. Maddie had no doubt her grandmother would make it to Nick. She had to give Nick time to get to the lake. He could drive and be there in five minutes. Unfortunately, he would be on the opposite side from where she was. There was only one place to park out there. The thought gave Maddie pause: Should she try to swim across the lake?

The nights were warmer than even a few weeks before but still chilly. Summer was close, and forecasters had even predicted an early hot stretch for the following week, but Willow Lake would be freezing. It never warmed up until mid-summer. Maddie was worried she would get hypothermia from the water. Of course, it was better to risk freezing than to let a madman stab her to death.

Maddie didn't allow herself time to worry. She figured she could make the decision on risking a swim when she got there. As it was now, she could hear her stalker tumbling through the brush as he tried to keep up. He wasn't far behind, but Maddie had managed to put some distance between them.

She cut hard to her left and jumped, knowing exactly where the large rock she and Nick used to draw on with chalk was located. She also knew there was a small indentation in the ground there. If she was lucky, the man wouldn't know and a fall would slow him.

Years of running five miles a day had kept Maddie in shape. She wasn't worried about running out of fuel, merely about what would happen if she got to the lake before Nick. How long would it take him?

Maddie heard a thud behind her, and she risked a glance over her shoulder. Her pursuer had tripped when he tried to run around the rock. Maddie turned back, a branch catching her cheek as she focused on the ground in front of her. She would be at the lake within minutes. Then she had a choice in front of her.

NICK WASN'T sure what to do. If he went to Maddie's house and tried to follow her on foot, he would be woefully behind. If he drove to the lake and parked, the water would separate them. Still, the lights of his police cruiser might be enough to dissuade whoever was following her.

Nick made his decision quickly, accelerating down the dirt road that led to the lake. He had to see her as soon as possible. Even if he couldn't touch her, seeing her would most certainly relieve the pressure building in his chest.

SHE'D MADE it to the lake, but the darkness on the northern shore told her Nick hadn't arrived yet. What had she expected? He didn't have his own personal teleporter. She just had to be patient.

Maddie slipped into a small cluster of trees near the shore to catch her breath. Willow Lake was a lake in name only. It was really more of an exaggerated pond. The distance between the two shores was still significant – especially with water this cold.

"Maddie."

She froze when she heard the taunting voice. She kept her breathing shallow and pressed against one of the trees, peering around it. *He was here.* His tumble obviously hadn't done him any discernible harm. He was about fifteen feet away, his back to her, and he was scanning all the foliage next to the lake. Maddie took the opportunity to study him. Under the almost full moon, he wasn't hard to recognize.

Todd Winthrop.

I knew it, she muttered internally. She was never going to let Nick live this down.

"Oh, Maddie," Todd crooned. "Come out, come out wherever you are."

Maddie remained silent.

"Oh, now don't be like this, Maddie," Todd said. "Or, should I call you 'Mad?' Isn't that what your beloved Nick calls you?"

Maddie didn't dare move a muscle.

"I saw you earlier tonight," Todd said. "You were spying on me out at the greenhouse. If you wanted to see me, all you had to do was ask. I'm more than willing to scratch the itch Nick refuses to attend to."

Todd waited.

"Oh, come on, Maddie," Todd said, stalking to the bushes nearest the lake and ripping through them angrily. "I don't have time to play games with you."

Maddie had so many questions she was tempted to break the silence. She knew it was a mistake, though.

"How much time do you think you have, Maddie? I'm guessing you have less time than Sarah Alden."

Maddie shifted silently. It was only a matter of time before Todd checked out the trees. She needed to find a different hiding spot. When she turned, she came face to face with another figure in the dark. This one was equally strong, if not as well built, and when the glittering eyes met hers under the dim light, Maddie inadvertently screamed.

"There you are," Todd said, turning swiftly.

"I've got her."

Terror washed over Maddie as she recognized the second figure. "Dustin?"

NICK SLAMMED his cruiser into park on the side of the road. The lights were flashing brightly, but he was not in the lake's parking lot. Something inside of him rebelled against that. He didn't know how, but he was sure it would be a mistake. So, instead, he parked as close to the southern shore as possible. He was going to have to brave the dark woods – sections he wasn't familiar with – and find Maddie that way.

"I'm coming, Mad," he muttered.

He paused when he heard a slight whispering. If he didn't know better, he could've sworn it sounded like Olivia. She was beckoning to him. Instead of questioning the sensation, he embraced it. If anyone could get him to Maddie in time, it was the mother who loved her more than anything.

"Lead me to her, Olivia," he said. "Hurry."

"I DON'T UNDERSTAND," Maddie said, ripping her arm away from Dustin and taking a step back.

Dustin didn't appear too concerned with Maddie's reaction. It's not like she had anywhere to go but the water, and as far as he was concerned, she'd never brave escape that way. He didn't know what Maddie did: Nick was coming.

"What took you so long?" Todd snapped. "Did the grandmother give you problems?"

"I don't have the grandmother," Dustin said.

"But … ."

"She was in the car and gone before I could get to her," Dustin explained. "I thought we were here for this one. I certainly don't want to play with the old one."

"Yes, but Maude knows someone was there," Todd countered. "She saw me in the driveway."

"Did she recognize you?"

"Not from that distance."

"So, what does it matter?" Dustin was nonplussed.

"Where do you think Maude drove to?"

"The senior center?"

Todd smacked the back of Dustin's head irritably. "She went straight to the police department, you moron."

"So? They don't even staff that thing at night."

"Yes, but Winters will move mountains to get to Maddie," Todd replied. "Think!"

"So, he's not out here now," Dustin said. "He can't possibly know where she ran."

"That's all we have going for us right now."

"What is the deal with you two," Maddie asked. "Why are you doing this?"

"Oh, you're asking the wrong questions, Maddie," Todd said. "What you should be asking is why we didn't start doing this sooner."

"How do you even know each other?"

"Dustin does some work out at Uncle Henry's greenhouse from time to time," Todd said. "I was out there visiting my cousin one day, and Dustin and I got to talking, and ... well ... one thing led to another."

"Oh, really, how does that conversation go? 'So, do you want to find a woman to murder tonight?'"

Todd chuckled appreciatively. "It took a few beers."

"So you're giving alcohol to minors, too? That's great. You're a real catch. I can't believe anyone would ever throw you back." Maddie knew antagonizing Todd wasn't in her best interests, but she was so confused she couldn't wrap her head around Dustin's appearance.

"Dustin is a good boy," Todd said. "Just like I was a good boy. That didn't stop bitches like you from thinking you were too good for me, though, did it?"

Maddie was flummoxed. "What are you talking about?"

"Oh, don't do that," Todd sneered. "I must've asked you out fifty times in high school."

"You only asked me out to upset Nick," Maddie protested.

"Are you stupid? As much as I like annoying Winters, I wanted you. Everyone wanted you. You were gawky and geeky in middle school, but you were smoking hot by the time high school hit. Do you really think Nick was why I asked you out?"

Maddie nodded, flustered. "What could you have possibly seen in me?"

"You're either delusional or blind," Todd replied. "Do you not know what you look like?"

"I ... ." Uncomfortable, Maddie shifted her attention to Dustin. "Why would you do this? You're the new king. That's what Christy said. You're the boy everyone wants, just like ... ."

"I was," Todd finished. "That's not as much fun as you might think. When you're the king, you can't give in to certain ... appetites."

Maddie felt sick.

"Word gets around in a small town," he continued. "I couldn't play the games I wanted to play with the girls in Blackstone Bay. That's why I had to start shopping out of town."

That explained Sarah Alden's confusion, Maddie mused. "Did you find Sarah at the greenhouse?"

"Good guess," Todd said. "She was out there looking for some flowers to plant. She was talking to Uncle Henry, and I saw her across the aisles, and I just knew I had to have her.

"I couldn't take her right away, of course," Todd said. "I pointed her out to Dustin, though, and he agreed she was the type of peach who needed to be plucked. So, we formed a plan."

"And what plan was that?"

"Well, I charmed her, of course," Todd said. "I talked her up. I told her how great my uncle's greenhouse was. I made inane chitchat about what plants work in this climate. I never thought Carrie's ramblings at family events would ever work to my advantage, but they did.

"When it came time for Sarah to leave, I invited her out to

dinner," he said. "She was thrilled to go out with me. I mean, who wouldn't be? I'm young and successful. I've never been married. I own my own business, for crying out loud."

"Yeah, you're a catch," Maddie mumbled.

"I took Sarah out to a nice restaurant on the bay," Todd said, ignoring Maddie's sarcasm. "She ordered the lobster."

Maddie's stomach rolled.

"She was polite enough to have red wine, though, and that allowed me to slip a little something into her drink," Todd said. "Nothing much. I don't like women when they're passed out. I just wanted her to be more ... pliable."

"That's why you wanted me to have the wine," Maddie said.

"It is," Todd said. "The second I knew you were back in town, I knew I had to have you. You denied me all through high school. There was no way I was going to let you deny me again."

"Where did you take Sarah after dinner?" Maddie was terrified, and also curious. If she stalled long enough, Nick would find her. He wouldn't abandon her. She knew that now.

"We took her to Dustin's place," Todd said. "His parents were out of town, and he was eager to have some fun of his own."

Dustin nodded enthusiastically. "She was awesome. You should've heard the way she moaned and cried. She loved it."

"I still don't understand why you did this, Dustin," Maddie said. "You're young. You have the world at your fingertips."

"Didn't you hear your friend the other night?" Dustin asked. "That red-headed devil told you exactly why I did this. My grades aren't good enough to get me into anything other than community college. I'm the football star, but no colleges are recruiting me. In a few years, I'm going to be nothing. I wanted to live now."

Maddie swallowed hard, her mind buzzing. "Does Henry know about this?"

"My uncle? Are you kidding? He's too soft," Todd said. "Apparently he had some *incident* when he was younger and stalked some woman. He claims he was out of control, but I figure that it must run in the family. That's what I'm going to use as a defense if I ever get caught, by the way."

"I'm sure you don't think you're going to get caught," Maddie said.

"Oh, I won't," Todd said. "Who would ever suspect me?"

"Nick does."

"No, Nick wants to suspect me," Todd corrected. "He knows he can never make an accusation against me, though. Our past makes that impossible. People will just think it's sour grapes. Besides, you and I broke up. What would my motive be?"

"We were never dating," Maddie countered. "You can't break up with someone you were never dating."

"That just looks better for me," Todd said. He hunkered his tall frame down so he could meet Maddie's terrified countenance on an even level. "What do you think, Mad? Will Nick kill himself when your body is discovered? He's been pining away for you for years. I know he's convinced himself you two will end up together, even if he's not ready to admit it yet. When I take that away from him, what will he be left with?"

"You're sick."

"I'm enthusiastic," Todd countered. "Speaking of that, I think we'd better get this show on the road."

"You want to do it here?" Dustin asked, unconvinced. "It's cold."

"They're going to search my house," Todd replied. "Your parents are home. Where else should we take her?"

"I'm not sure," Dustin hedged. "It's just so cold. I'm not even sure I'll be able to ... you know."

"Oh, grow up," Todd scoffed. "Once she's naked, you won't be able to think of anything but taking her. Trust me. Her body is fantastic."

Maddie was out of time, and she knew it. There was only one thing she could do now. Without thinking of the consequences, Maddie lifted her leg and slammed it into Todd's exposed crotch. He doubled over, screaming as the pain washed over him. Dustin was so surprised, he froze in place.

Maddie took advantage of the few precious seconds she had and launched herself into the water. It was freezing, but it was her only option. She kicked out hard and stroked. If she was lucky, she'd make it to the other side of the lake before passing out.

If she wasn't, well, anything was better than what they had planned.

NICK WAS sure he heard a scream. He increased his pace, and when he crested the hill and dropped onto the sandy beach, it took him a second to register what he was seeing.

Todd was doubled over and holding his groin. The other figure, one Nick recognized as Dustin Bishop without realizing the ramifications of what he was seeing, was standing next to Todd and waiting for instructions. There was no sign of Maddie.

"Get her!"

"No way," Dustin said. "Do you know how cold that water must be?"

Nick shifted his head, scanning the water. It was dark, but he could see a small blob bobbing in the middle of the lake. *Maddie.*

"We have to get her," Todd said. "If she escapes, she'll tell Winters what we did."

"I think I already know."

Todd and Dustin both shifted at the same time. Nick was gratified to see the fear on Dustin's face. The sheer hatred on Todd's gave him pause.

"Why am I not surprised? I should've known Maddie's great protector would come for her."

Nick trudged closer to them. He kept his gun holstered. He didn't want to give either of them a reason to panic. He knew Maddie couldn't last long in the water, though. This had to end – and it had to end quickly. "I want you both to disarm yourselves and put your hands in the air."

"And what if we don't?" Todd asked.

"Then I'll kill you."

"Oh, whatever." Todd was beside himself. "You've never killed anyone. It's not as easy as you think."

"I'm willing to kill you," Nick said. "I think you've earned it."

"Oh, and what about young Dustin here? Are you going to kill him, too?"

"I'm going to arrest him."

"Oh, I don't know," Todd said. "Can you take us both out before your precious Maddie freezes to death?"

That was the question, wasn't it? Nick reached for his gun, but it was too late, they were both rushing him at the same time. Nick didn't think, he just reacted. Dustin got to him first, and he laid the teenager out with a quick punch to the face. His swing was short but strong, and the teen hit the ground hard.

If Todd was scared by the turn of events, he didn't show it. He only slowed momentarily before launching himself on Nick. "I'm going to kill you!"

MADDIE WAS DROWNING. The cold water sent her body into shock, and black clouds were poking at the edges of her mind. Nick was grappling with Todd while Dustin lay unmoving at his feet, but they seemed really far away. Maddie's feet were still treading water, but they were slowing.

"You have to get out of the water, Maddie."

Maddie shifted, her mother's concerned face wafting into view. "I'm … tired, Mommy."

"You have to swim back to the shore," Olivia ordered. "You have to do it now. You don't have a lot of time."

"I'm not sure I can."

"Madeline Graves, you can do anything you set your mind to," Olivia said sternly. "You need to swim to the shore. Nick is there. He's waiting for you."

"Nicky," Maddie mumbled.

"Swim!"

Maddie tried to move. She really did. She felt as if her muscles were on fire, though, and instead she started sinking. She wasn't going to make it.

As the cold water enveloped her, and her head slipped under the water, Maddie's last thought was of Nick. *I love you.*

NICK SLAMMED his fist into Todd's face as hard as he could. He heard the unmistakable sound of bones breaking as Todd crumpled to the ground. Instead of cuffing him, like he should have, Nick turned his attention to the water just in time to see Maddie's head slip underneath. "Maddie!"

Nick raced toward the water, all thoughts of proper police procedure and possible prisoner escape fleeing. He had to get to her.

He plunged into the water, forcing thoughts of the bitter cold out of his mind. He kicked hard, making it to the spot where he'd last seen Maddie quickly. He dove under the water, searching the murky depths. He splayed his hands out in the dark – his fingers brushing against something waving in the depths. *Her hair!* He kicked harder, and this time his hand found her jacket. He tugged her to him, the two of them emerging from the shallows at the same time.

"Winters?"

It was Dale Kreskin. He was standing on the shore, his gun trained on Dustin and Todd. Nick had no idea when he'd arrived. He was just happy to see him. "Get an ambulance," he croaked.

"Is she ... ?"

"Get an ambulance!"

Nick managed to swim to the shore, even though his strength was waning with each cold stroke. It took everything he had to pull Maddie's limp form from the water, and Kreskin ultimately had to help him. Nick held her close as he checked to see if she was breathing. When he couldn't detect any warmth on her lips, he laid her flat on the ground and started pumping her chest.

"Don't you dare think of leaving me again," Nick ordered. "You're not leaving me."

"Winters, you should let me do that," Kreskin said. "You're going into shock."

"You're not leaving me again, Maddie," Nick said, lowering his mouth to hers and pinching her nose so he could fill her lungs with oxygen. "You're not leaving me!"

Maddie's body convulsed suddenly, water spewing out her lungs. Nick cried out, relief washing over him. He tilted her body to the side. "Get it out, Mad. Get it out."

When she was done, Nick shifted her body so it was flush with his and he wrapped his arms around her tightly. Maddie was confused, her eyes distant, but she recognized him. "Nicky."

"It's okay," he said, rocking her. "It's okay. Everything is going to be okay. I promise. Everything is going to be okay."

Maddie was too tired to put up a fight. "Nicky," she murmured, unconsciousness claiming her again.

Nick pressed his lips to her frigid forehead. "Everything is going to be okay."

27. TWENTY-SEVEN

"Sir, you've got to give her to us."

Nick clutched Maddie to his chest, the doctor's words confusing him. "She needs me."

"Sir, she needs to be admitted and warmed," the doctor said. "You need to hand her over."

Instead of waiting for the ambulance, Kreskin had piled Todd and Dustin into the back of his cruiser and herded an increasingly erratic Nick into the passenger seat. Nick had held onto Maddie so hard during the drive, Kreskin was worried he was smothering her.

When they arrived at the hospital, the doctors immediately tried to take Maddie from Nick – but he was fighting their efforts.

Kreskin grabbed Nick's shoulders forcefully. "Winters, she needs help. I know you don't want to let her go, but these doctors are here to help her. Hand her over."

In the back of his mind, Nick grasped the seriousness of the words. He reluctantly rested Maddie on the gurney in front of him. "I don't know how long she was in the water."

"How long were you in the water, sir?"

"I'm ... fine."

"He's in shock or something," Kreskin supplied.

"I'm not in shock," Nick protested.

"You're shaking like a leaf, man," Kreskin said. "You should've waited for help to go in after her."

"I think he's showing signs of hypothermia," one of the nurses said, flashing a light in Nick's eyes.

"I'm fine," Nick said, pushing her hand away. He was confused. He just knew he had to make sure Maddie was okay. He couldn't let himself rest until he knew.

"Admit him," the doctor ordered. "I don't care if it's against his wishes. We can't let the new town hero die on the eve of his big debut."

"I need to be with Maddie," Nick muttered.

He didn't have the strength to fight when two nurses and two orderlies forced him onto a separate gurney. "She'll be fine," one of the nurses said.

"Maddie."

Nick was losing consciousness, but he was still alert enough to recognize a familiar face when it dropped down to brush an invisible kiss against his cheek. "She'll be okay, Nick," Olivia said. "I'll be with her."

"Maddie."

WHEN NICK WOKE HOURS LATER, he felt as if his whole body was on fire. He was in a hospital room, and he was alone. It took a few moments for the night's events to come into focus.

"Maddie."

He rolled off the bed, scowling when he realized his police uniform had been replaced with a hospital gown. When he made his way to the hallway, he found Kreskin resting on a chair outside of his room. "Where is she?"

Kreskin's eyes snapped open. "You look better."

"Where is she?"

"You don't look good, but you look better."

Kreskin was smiling, and the expression irritated Nick beyond measure. "Where is she?"

"So, hero, how are you feeling?"

Kreskin was purposely avoiding Nick's question, which was enough to make him panic. "Did she ... ?" *She couldn't be dead.*

"She's fine," Kreskin said, patting his arm reassuringly. "The doctors want to keep her overnight. Her grandmother is in with her now. She hasn't woken up. They gave her a sedative to make sure she would get the rest she needs. They wanted to give you one, too, but I didn't want to face you tomorrow if they did."

She was okay. Nick exhaled heavily. "What happened to Todd and Dustin?" Much of the night was a blur, but Nick hadn't forgotten finding the two of them next to the lake.

"They've been taken into custody," Kreskin replied. "We're questioning them in the morning. I figured you'd want to be there for that. Dustin was singing a pretty song in the car, though. He's blaming everything on Todd. He says he was coerced."

"They're both assholes."

"They are," Kreskin agreed. "The state police are coming to help. We have them searching Winthrop's townhouse and Dustin's parents' house. We had to wake the judge up, but when we told him what happened, he signed the search warrants without complaint. He says he wants updates."

"Did they say why they killed Sarah Alden?"

"As far as I can tell, it was out of boredom." Kreskin didn't seem any more thrilled with the explanation than Nick was.

"What about Maddie? Did they say why they went after her?"

"They saw her at the greenhouse tonight," Kreskin said. "They thought she knew."

Nick rubbed his forehead wearily. "How is Maude?"

"Feisty."

"Is she ... is she okay? Maddie is all she has left. She loves her."

"I don't think Maude is the only one," Kreskin said, his face serious. "By the way, Cassidy is in the waiting room. She's been demanding to see you, but ... ."

"I don't want to see her."

"I figured," Kreskin said. "You're going to have to deal with that situation. You know that, right?"

"I can't deal with it now," Nick said. "I need to see Maddie."

"How did I know that you were going to say that?" Kreskin led Nick down the hallway. "She's in there. She's not going to wake up tonight. They drugged her. She kept calling for you and ... well ... her mother. I think she was just confused."

Nick's mind flooded with the memory of Olivia's voice as she led him – not one misstep – to Maddie. "Yeah, she's probably just confused. She'll be fine in the morning."

"You're going to sit with her all night, aren't you?"

"Yes."

Maude was asleep in a chair when Nick entered the room. He was quiet. He didn't want to wake her. She'd had a long night, and she would spend days doting on Maddie.

He made his way to Maddie's bed and studied her face. She looked content. Her face was pale, but there was a small smile playing at the corner of her lips. *Was she dreaming of him?*

Nick lowered his mouth to Maddie's forehead and pressed his lips to it. He was relieved to find warmth there instead of cold. "I'll be right here, Mad."

"Of course you will."

This time, Nick was sure it was Olivia's voice he was hearing. "We'll all be here," he said, kissing her forehead again. "Everything is going to be okay. I promise."

From her spot next to Maude, Olivia couldn't help but smile. Things were falling into place. Maddie was going to be happy. She was sure of it. "Goodnight, Mom," she said, lowering her mouth to Maude's ear. "Take care of our Maddie. Oh, and don't forget to take care of Nick, too. They're about to go on a bumpy ride together."

Maude didn't answer, but her mouth slid into a sly smile.

"It will be bumpy," Olivia whispered. "It's going to be wonderful, too. Just you wait and see."

Made in the USA
Las Vegas, NV
30 April 2024